RETURN OF THE FAST GUN

RETURN OF THE FAST GUN

LAURAN PAINE

THORNDIKE
CHIVERS

This Large Print edition is published by Thorndike Press, Waterville, Maine, USA and by BBC Audiobooks Ltd, Bath, England.
Thorndike Press is an imprint of The Gale Group.
Thorndike is a trademark and used herein under license.
The text of this Large Print edition is unabridged.
Other aspects of the book may vary from the original edition.
Set in 16 pt. Plantin.

LIBRARY OF CONGRESS CATALOGING-IN-PUBLICATION DATA

Paine, Lauran.
  Return of the fast gun / by Lauran Paine.
    p. cm.
  Originally published in 1961 under the pen name of John Kilgore.
  ISBN-13: 978-0-7862-9952-2 (hardcover : alk. paper)
  ISBN-10: 0-7862-9952-5 (hardcover : alk. paper)
  1. Large type books. I. Title.
PS3566.A34R47 2007
813'.54—dc22   2007033974

BRITISH LIBRARY CATALOGUING-IN-PUBLICATION DATA AVAILABLE

Published in 2007 in the U.S. by arrangement with Golden West Literary Agency.
Published in 2008 in the U.K. by arrangement with The Golden West Literary Agency.

U.K. Hardcover: 978 1 405 64354 2 (Chivers Large Print)
U.K. Softcover: 978 1 405 64355 9 (Camden Large Print)

Printed in the United States of America on permanent paper
10 9 8 7 6 5 4 3 2 1

RETURN OF THE FAST GUN

CHAPTER ONE

"Hold it! Just sit up there on your horse and don't move."

For the space of several seconds there was only an echo to the stillness, to the fretwork-shade in among the trees. Then a lean shadow holding a carbine stepped into full view. There was a shell-belt and pistol on his right hip. He stared up at the rider a moment, then he squinted; screwed up a boyish face and peered hard, and his mouth dropped open.

"Well; for God's sake . . . Aren't you Ben Roan?"

The mounted man seemed deaf. His tanned skin, tight-drawn and smooth, showed flawlessly calm over the flat planes of his face. His eyes, like blue ice, were hard on the youth and his carbine. He said nothing, and the boy shifted his grip on the carbine and repeated his name.

"Ben Roan . . ."

"Were you expecting President Grant?"

The youth swallowed and flushed. "You can't go no farther," he said. "The trail's closed from here on."

Roan's wide blue eyes lifted from the lad's face, went up the trail a ways, then lowered again. "Why?" he asked.

"Closed from our place onwards."

"The hell it is," Roan said softly. "Who says it is?"

"Us."

Roan leaned back in the saddle. He wasn't more than average height, but there was a durable squareness to him. "You'd be Guy, wouldn't you — the youngest Marlow?"

"I'm Guy — yes."

"Well now, Guy," Roan said quietly, "when I left this country you weren't more'n sixteen. You were a pretty decent kid." Roan paused a moment. "Let's keep it like that, shall we?"

"What're you getting at?"

Roan nodded his head up the trail. "I'm going on up," he said, "I don't want to fight, Guy, but I'm going on up to the old home place." Guy's jaw set in a stubborn way. Roan noticed and was briefly silent, then he asked casually, "How're your brothers, and the Old Man?"

Guy's hard look lingered. He was resolute,

but he was also scared; Ben Roan was a legend, with a reputation as long as your arm. "They're all right," he said, "and you still can't go on up."

Roan nodded thoughtfully, then he said, "I don't want to fight you, Guy. Move off to my left a ways. Go on; I'm not going to ride past, I'm going to show you how easy it would be for me to drop you even with that gun in your hand. Go on, Guy . . . A little farther. Now you see it, don't you? That gun's cocked; it's been on you ever since you first stopped me. That's the first thing a man learns, Guy — notice which side a man wears his gun on. When you throw down on him — be on that side. Now then; you see that big oak gall where you were standing . . . ?" There was no perceptible movement, but a flat short-gun blast broke the stillness and the oak gall burst with a puff of acrid, brown dust. When Guy looked back both Roan's hands were lying lightly on the saddlehorn. Sweat prickled his shoulders.

"That was fast," he said.

Roan nodded. "Fast enough, Guy. Another thing a man learns: cock your gun when you throw down on someone. I could have pegged you before you could have got off a shot." The steady blue eyes were unwavering. "Now listen, Guy; there's been enough trouble up in here; let's you and me start off on the right foot, what say?"

"The Old Man says no one's to go past."

"You know cussed well I've got a right up there," Roan replied with quiet patience. "You know the old Roan place is mine."

"You been away a long time, Ben. Thing's have changed. We got squatters' rights up there now."

"The Old Man say that?"

"Yes."

"He's wrong, Guy; dead wrong. I been paying the taxes these past six years. The title's in my name and it's good. Now, Guy, you go tell your paw I'm back; and I don't want anyone down here closing the road up to my place."

Guy looked at the horseman and knew what his father would say about the return of Ben Roan; about Guy letting him pass. The carbine's forearm was slippery with sweat. Guy knew he wasn't going to oppose Roan's passage. He swore to himself; *why didn't El or Hal ride up?*

"Pump the shells out of the carbine, Guy. I don't expect you'd pot a man in the back, but six years is a long time; folks change, sometimes."

Guy obeyed with stinging eyes.

10

"Now the pistol."

When both guns were empty Roan lifted the reins. There was neither triumph nor antagonism in his gaze. "You're welcome up at my place any time you take a notion to ride up," he said.

Guy watched him ride up the trail. There were actual tears in his eyes then; tears of humiliation. Ben Roan disappeared around a bend, the sound of his passing dwindled and died. Guy squatted, began chucking shells back into his guns, and cursing.

The trail was weed-grown, dappled with sunlight, dusty and metallic smelling with summer's hot scorch. Ben Roan felt twice-experienced pain as he rode over it. He paused beside a puddling spot where seepage water oozed from rocks, remembering how, as a small boy, he had sat there by the hour, hands clasped tightly around his legs, watching tadpoles.

Farther up, where the trail twisted and turned, he relied on memory, faint though awakening, to carry him over the unmarked, grassy spots. No wagons had been up there in years; the trail ran out in the grass. He followed it, seeking familiar landmarks; there were some, but not many. Over two ridges and down along the edge of an emerald meadow it went, very faintly outlined. Across a hurrying creek with grey stones in its bed, and where trout-minnows scurried frantically away from his shadow.

Up through another span of meadows and there it was. Only it wasn't. The site was there; the indentations in the earth, and the remembered places, like the twin cotton-woods bending southward where a man with big hands had once fashioned a rope-swing in the golden-yellow days of a warm autumn.

It was all there but the house and barn. A char there, rusted metal here. A hasp, a splinter of white crockery in the tall-bending grass. Broken corral poles, sagging gates, pieces of boards lying like old bones, bleached and curled, where others had torn down the buildings for wood.

He rode past; as far as the broken paling-fence with its slanting, grey headboard with the knothole in it. That was his father's grave — Eb Roan. Next to his father was a straighter, primmer looking slab — his mother. He dismounted and let the chestnut horse drag his reins, grazing. He moved into the filigreed pattern of shade from a twisted, un-cared for apple tree, and there he sank down on the warm earth.

Sat there with his pain, knowing both hurt and peacefulness at the same time. He was home. He had come back. He was sitting there in the past.

He got up finally, dusted the seat of his breeches off and walked aimlessly through the shade where the house had been; where he had been born, and wondered again, for the hundredth time, how the sickness had ever got this far back, to carry off both his parents? Why hadn't it taken him, too; he'd been pretty young then. No; not really young — not in years. Young in everything *but* years. In those days the world began at the house and ended at the rim of the meadow. He'd been content to ride with his paw and salt the cattle, to round-up, and once, to trail them down to Deming where he'd trembled with excitement, at the size and smell of a city; anxious to get there, to see, then more anxious to get home. Young only in living, in experience . . .

This had been the only solid, permanent thing he'd known, before his parents were taken off, and in the years after it had remained a shrine in his heart. There'd been times when he'd gone hungry to pay the taxes, but he'd done it.

Memories, pain, and stillness. After an hour he caught the horse and rode away, and turned once, atop a windswept ridge to look back. The afternoon was mellow, like the hush back down there. He felt it; it went into him like a knife and lingered there.

Riding southerly along the ridge he gazed out over the land. It was big and sere with nodding tufted heads of bunch-grass bending drowsily before a ground-ripple of air. There were spindly willows along creek beds, and dark squares with swishing tails among them; cattle. Distantly he could hear an occasional lowing; the soft call of cows and the broken, insistent, repetitious bellow of rutting bulls.

He arrived in Deming late in the afternoon. Puddling dust squirted upwards from his horse's hooves, dulling the sound of his passage. The village was heat-drowsy and languid. Even the liverybarn hostler, seamed and shrivelled with age, was listless when he took Roan's chestnut and led it deep into the barn, with loose reins flopping.

At the Oases Saloon Ben ran into a man he remembered; Joel Partin, the blacksmith. Partin kept studying him in the back-bar mirror, and his glance was troubled.

"Can't place me, can you?" Ben said affably.

"No, sir, I can't, and it's bothersome."

"Ben Roan."

Partin's lids swept up. "Well," he said in a way that was emphatic astonishment. "Well

14

sure; I recollect now. Well; it's been quite a spell, indeed it has."

"Little over six years."

Partin nodded soberly at his glass of beer and said nothing. His brows were drawing down in thought.

"Town seems the same."

"Yes. Well; Deming don't change much."

"Same stores, same dry desert," Ben said. "It doesn't seem like six years since I left here."

"I remember," Partin said. "I recollect all right. I felt sort of mean the day they put you on the stage for Socorro. You was scared stiff." Partin hooked a foot over the rail and nodded distantly. "Guess I knew more how you felt than most folks did. When I was a button it happened about the same way to me. My folks got killed in '49. I got shipped to shirt-tail relatives too. I've never forgot that hollow feeling I had in the belly, either. Plumb scared stiff."

"Another beer?"

Partin shook his head. "No thanks, I got to get back. Work's piled up on me."

Ben watched the blacksmith cross the drowsy room and press out past the doors. Over the back-bar was a mounted Long-horn's head. The wicked sweep of horns glistened above vicious glass eyes. It looked

15

as though the head was being held purposely high, above the strong-smelling room below. He smiled at his thoughts.

Ben Roan was still standing there a half hour later when Deputy Marshal Cliff Thompson entered. Being an observant and deceptively mild mannered man, Thompson had no trouble selecting Ben Roan from the other lazing patrons of the Oases. He went up to the bar, leaned on it, and nodded for a beer. When it arrived he half-turned and said, "My name's Cliff Thompson; deputy U.S. Marshal hereabouts."

"Ben Roan."

Their hands touched briefly and fell away. In the back of Ben's mind a suspicion formed up.

"I've heard of you," Thompson said. "Care for another beer?"

"No, thanks."

"You'd be Eb Roan's son, wouldn't you?"

"That's right."

"And the same Ben Roan folks call the fastest gun in New Mexico Territory."

Ben's eyes crinkled slightly. "How do I answer that," he said. "One way'd make a blow-hard, the other way'd make me tell you I'd never heard that said — and that'd be a lie."

Thompson smiled. For a moment he

16

didn't speak, then he said, "It's a change to meet a fast-gun who backs off from bragging."

"Maybe," Ben said dryly, "you shouldn't put too much faith in what Joel Partin says."

Thompson's grin broadened. "I don't; but it wasn't only Joel." Thompson drained his glass and set it down. "You see, I had some other callers, earlier; the Marlows."

Ben's glance hardened. "They must have ridden hard," he said.

"They did. All three boys and old Will. Seems there's some question of title on your folks' homestead up in the foothills."

Anger moved slightly in Ben. "No question at all, Marshal. I kept up the taxes. Go look at the records."

"I already did that."

"And?"

"You kept things up all right, but there's never been a transfer from the original owners."

"That doesn't amount to much. I aim to take care of that today."

Thompson inclined his head thoughtfully. "No, that doesn't amount to much."

Ben studied Thompson's face. "What else is on your mind, then?"

"Trouble. Trouble with the Marlows. You see, they got a notion about squatters' rights up there."

"I know. I rode into some of that this morning. Guy was blocking the trail with a carbine. He had no right, of course, but remembering his paw, I can understand how it happened."

"Did you know the Marlows very well?" Thompson asked.

"Passably well. When we were kids Will wouldn't let the two older boys, El and Hal, come up to our place. Guy was younger then; I didn't know him as well as the others."

"Did your paw ever have trouble with them over the road up the draw to your place?"

"No," Ben said. "My paw didn't have trouble with folks."

"But the road's across a corner of the Marlow place. Didn't Will try to close it in those days?"

Ben shook his head. "He never tried to. If he had he'd have had a cougar by the tail. He knew that. Like I said, my paw didn't have trouble with folks — they knew him."

Thompson concentrated on a brown-paper cigarette he was twisting up. "I've heard your paw was quite a man," he said, popped the cigarette into his mouth, lit it and exhaled.

Ben said nothing. He was staring at the bar-top. When Thompson sighed he looked up. "I don't think there'll be any trouble," he said.

The Marshal gazed critically at Ben. "Things seem pretty much the same hereabouts, don't they?"

"Pretty much, yes."

"Well; folks change."

Ben straightened off the bar. "Listen, Marshal," he said, wearying of the conversation. "You can quit worrying. I didn't come back to make any trouble."

"But you didn't come back to avoid it either, did you?"

"No."

"Why *did* you come back, Roan?"

"To settle down."

"Up there?"

"Yes."

"But there's nothing up there."

"I know that. I can guess who tore down the house and barn and carted off the lumber. I expected as much. It usually happens around deserted places. I'll build a new house; and I always thought the barn should've been closer to the creek anyway. It used to get afternoon sun in the summertime and be hot enough inside to boil owls."

"And run cattle up there?"

19

"Yes."

Marshal Thompson sighed again, louder. "Old Will Marlow isn't going to take that smiling."

"Maybe not, but as long as that place is mine I aim to settle down there."

"He'd buy it from you, Roan."

"It's not for sale, but if it was he'd offer me one year's taxes for it — I know how cowmen buy abandoned ranches, Marshal."

"About that road . . . There's some question whether the right-of-way still exists. It hasn't been used for nearly seven years. Marlow saw a lawyer about it."

Ben's forehead creased the slightest bit. "That road's been used since I was a little kid."

"But it hasn't been in *continuous* use."

"What of it; a road's a road."

"I'm not too clear about this," Thompson said, "but unless a road's being used, or has been used lately, folks owning land it crosses can petition to have it abandoned, and close it."

"I never heard that before."

"Better see a lawyer about it. No sense in walking into trouble half-cocked."

Ben's face darkened. He looked steadily at Thompson without speaking, then turned and walked out of the saloon.

Summer twilight was settling. Far out, the sun hung on a jagged snag of mountain like a punctured egg yolk; red flowed outward and downward from it. A little evening breeze scrabbled along Deming's rooftops rattling shingles; it was refreshing.

People drifted past. Down the road and across the way a richly musical sound clanged from Joel Partin's smithy. Closer, a raffish hound-dog sniffed at an overhang-up-right and a day-dreaming boy made squiggly marks in the dust with a crooked stick.

Ben watched a horse-mule and an old mare tooth-duelling across a pole at the public water trough down by the liverybarn. A cowboy rode past, dismounted before the barn's maw and stood there peering into the shadows for the hostler. When he finally called out his voice sounded scratchy with annoyance.

Ben absorbed both sound and movement without heeding either. His mind had resurrected Will Marlow's face; had closed down around it. Elbert and Harold were less distinct, but he remembered them. It was old Will's face that stood out; his face and the rest of him; stringy, slack, and weasel-like. Hard around the mouth, treacherous around the eyes.

Better see a lawyer about it . . .

He went down the walk to a diner crowded between Ewell's Saddle & Harness Shop, and F. Burton's Land & Cattle Company, ate supper, made a cigarette and smoked it while gazing around at the other diners. When darkness finally came someone went around the room lighting lamps; the smell of coal oil mingled with the scent of food. Ben paid and went back outside. Most of his anger had died by then.

He considered riding up to the Marlow place and talking to the Old Man; knew it would be a waste of time and forgot it. Up the plankwalk a man was backing out of an office. He was slight of build and wore a handsome cinnamon-coloured derby. Above him hung a sign which read: 'Charles E. Bell, Lawyer.'

Ben watched Charles E. Bell snap the lock on his door and straighten up. Recalling Thompson's suggestion he decided no harm could come of talking to a lawyer.

"Excuse me," he said as Bell swung past. "Are you a lawyer?"

"I am, sir." Two bright, dark eyes looked up into Ben's face. "Can I help you?"

"It could wait until morning."

"No, no; walk along with me. We can talk on the way to my place."

Ben walked and talked. When they stepped down off the plankwalk and trudged through the dust of a side-road where houses sat, with gaps between them like openings in an uneven row of teeth, he had told the entire story. For a while Bell walked along in silence. At a sagging gate, once whitewashed, but dingy now and sagging, he stepped aside with a flourish. "Come in for a moment, Mr. Roan."

"Well," Ben hesitated in the gloom. "I don't want to interfere with your —"

"Nonsense, nonsense; never put off what can be taken care of at once. After you, sir."

The porch groaned when they crossed it. There were curtains criss-crossed over a window in the door, which Bell held open, and closed after himself. A hatrack made of pegs protruding from two interlocked wooden diamonds received the cinnamon derby, and Bell smiled for the first time.

"Here; sit here, Mr. Roan."

A girl came into the room and stopped dead-still in the doorway. Ben arose and Charles Bell beamed at her. "Come in, honey," he said. "I won't be long. Come over here. Fine. Mr. Roan, this is my daughter, Della. Honey, this is Mr. Ben Roan."

Ben bent slightly in the middle. "Glad to know you, ma'm," he said.

23

"Thank you, Mr. Roan. Will you have supper with us?"

"I'm obliged, ma'm, but I just finished eating."

She was tall; taller than her father in fact, and she was buxom and sturdy. Her eyes, dark like Bell's, looked straight out at you. Ben guessed her about nineteen years old.

"Can I get you both a cup of coffee, then?"

"Thank you, honey," Bell said, sitting down. "We'd like that. Now then, Mr. Roan, tell me — who is handling this case for the Marlows?"

"I don't know. I didn't know they'd talked to a lawyer until Marshal Thompson told me."

"I see; well, it doesn't make much difference."

"Is there anything to this business about a road being abandoned after it's been unused for six or seven years?"

"Yes; but I'll have to look it up before I'm sure exactly how long a road has to have been abandoned before it can be declared closed. That will be the backbone of our case, you see. That, and the extenuating circumstance that you were not able until this time, to use the road."

Bell's daughter returned with two cups of coffee on a little tray. Ben stood up to take his and said, "Thank you." She smiled up at him, a flash of perfect teeth in a beautiful face.

"Are you certain you couldn't find room for some roast beef, Mr. Roan?"

"I truly wish I could," he said, returning the smile.

She moved to her father's side. Bell took the cup absently and nodded his thanks. "I think you have a good case," he said to Ben, who remained standing until after the girl left the room, then wished he might leave, but because the coffee was too hot to gulp down in two swallows, he stood there in silence. "In the first place, Mr. Roan, dissenting landowners must be notified of an intention to condemn a right-of-way. That's so they can dissent in court. Of course there's a statute of limitations . . . I'm hazy about that, though," Bell looked up with a smile. "But all in all I think we have a good case." Ben nodded in silence, the lawyer sipped his coffee then said, "Roan, Roan. Where have I heard that name before?"

"It's fairly common," Ben said, and made the tired little joke he'd had jibed at him all his life. "Like the saying, 'Roan horses, wrong men'."

"Yes; roan horses . . . Is your family an old one in these parts?"

"Not any more. Like I told you, my folks died in the epidemic and I got shipped to in-laws at Socorro where I stayed a couple of years, then went out on my own. After I left, there weren't any Roans around Deming, I'm sure of that."

"Well; I've heard the name somewhere. Not that it matters," Bell said, arising.

"How long have you folks been in Deming?" Ben asked.

"Three years now. We came from Missouri. We left the year my wife died." The dark eyes grew ironic for a moment. "The law business isn't as brisk out here as it was back east. On the other hand a man's future is in the palm of his hand, out here. There's nothing to chain him to the yesterdays, Mr. Roan."

"No," Ben said, "I guess for folks like you there isn't." He put aside the coffee cup, promised to see Bell in a day or two, and left.

Uptown, there was music and noise coming from the saloons. Riders trotted through splashes of orange lamplight. People strolled past, faces faint and blurred. Marshal Thompson was smoking on a bench in front of Partin's Forge. He nodded at Ben and gestured to the bench. When Ben sank down Thompson exhaled a fragrant cloud of smoke that hung in the still night air. "Nice night," he said.

Ben grunted. "I saw a lawyer."

"Which one?"

"Feller named Bell. Know him?"

A nod; smoked drifted upwards, around the brim of Marshal Thompson's hat. "What'd he say?"

"That I had a good case; that Marlow had to petition a court to close that road, and I could protest — something like that."

"Sounds legal," Thompson said, stretching his long legs out in front of him and staring down them at his boot-toes. "What do you figure to do in the meantime?"

"Start building."

Thompson continued to study his boot-toes before he spoke again. "What if they try to keep you from going up there, like they did today?"

"I guess I'll just go on past," Ben replied.

"Don't suppose you'd take a room here in town until this is settled."

"Why should I?"

"To keep from getting killed — or from killing somebody."

Ben snorted. "I've known those Marlows since I was a button," he said. "They aren't the killing kind."

"Like I said before, Roan — folks change.

Maybe old Will's nothing to fret about, but El and Hal . . . I've been hereabouts five years, Roan, and maybe they weren't much when you were a kid, but they are now. Don't sell them short." Thompson held out his tobacco sack.

Ben shook his head and leaned back on the bench. "I never sell folks short, Marshal. That's why I'm still alive. What'd El and Hal ever do to make folks step wide around them?"

"Fight. The only one I've never had any trouble with is the youngest, Guy. The Old Man's a troublemaker; so are Elbert and Harold."

"Years back," Ben mused aloud, "folks thought of the Marlows as small-time nesters. No one dropped them a second look."

"Did they have many cattle in those days?"

"Not many," Ben answered. "About a hundred head maybe. Mangy, cross-bred critters. Paw and I used to chouse them off our graze whenever we came onto them up there. Old Will never put up any hay and every winter he'd lose a few head from starvation."

"They own a pretty nice herd now. Some say as many as five hundred good cows and bulls."

"I can guess how they got them," Ben said thinly.

Thompson acted like he hadn't heard. "The point is," he said, "I know cussed well what's going to happen the next time you ride up there. Will'll be watching for you. El and Hal'll be with him."

"I'll be looking a little out, too," Ben said dryly. "By the way, their old grandfather used to live with them . . . I expect he'd be dead by now, though."

"No; he's still there. Pretty feeble though. The last time I was up there he was out on the porch, in a bunk they built against the wall for him. I guess he was too stout to keep inside. You know how those old folks get . . ."

"Yeah." Ben stood up, sniffed the night, smelled creosote bush and curing grass and sun-baked earth. "You know," he said softly, "I thought coming back was going to be a lot different. Quiet and restful-like. I've been years thinking about this; about fixing up the place, running a few head, going fishing, hunting . . . Sort of letting the years roll by like that."

"You're not that old," Thompson said, squashing out his cigarette.

"No, but I've been a tumbleweed long enough. Drifting sort of wearies a man."

29

"I know. I was looking for a town to settle in, when I came up the trail from Texas." Thompson got up and hitched at his shell-belt. "Until you came along it was about like that, too. Quiet and lazy-like."

Ben scoffed. "You're seeing trouble where none exists . . . Not very much, anyway."

"Roan; if anyone's making a mistake, it's you. Twice now I've told you those Marlows've changed. They aren't at all like you remember them."

"That breed never changes."

"In some ways, no; in other ways, yes. They're troublesome — I reckon they've always been like that. But they aren't rock-ranchers any more, Roan. They've got good cattle, fast horses, and money. If you roil them up they're going to cut quite a swathe."

"Not over the Roan place they won't."

Cliff Thompson looked exasperated. "You're sure hard to convince. All right; stick to your notions. All I ask is that before you do anything, you make plumb certain you're in the right."

"I aim to. That's why I saw that lawyer. But if the Marlows are carrying a chip, why I expect they won't have too much trouble getting it knocked off."

An edge came to Thompson's voice. "I

wouldn't make that kind of talk if I was you. At least not until a court says you're in the right — then only if they make trouble."

Ben looked the marshal straight in the face. "There's such a thing as being too peaceable. I learnt that a long time ago. I also learnt the best way to keep guns from pointing at you, is to own a fast one."

"And you own it."

"Six years of proving it, Marshal, would make a sensible man think a little before he went on the prod."

"Should," Thompson said, "but it won't. Not the Marlows. I know."

Ben stepped down off the walk, strode at an angle across the road towards a solitary lantern glowing within a glass ball, with the word 'Rooms' lettered across it.

Upstairs, above the Oases Saloon with sound vibrating through the floor, Ben flung up the window and let night-scent come inside. Beyond Deming was a brooding stillness; a great sea of sage that made a dark and lumpy carpet across the desert.

Ben stood there gazing out. Strange how agitated lawmen got when they thought they smelled trouble coming. Stranger still, that a man as thoughtful-appearing as Thompson, should be so incorrect in his appraisal of the Marlows. What difference did it make if old Will did get his hackles up; he wasn't anybody and never had been. And Hal; lanky, unshorn, with a flake or two of nervous ferocity in the depths of his eyes. He'd never been more than two-thirds bluff.

Elbert used to be more like Ben; average in height, powerful, not given to lots of talk, and, for a Marlow, not particularly troublesome.

He turned away from the window, looked with distaste at the sagging iron bedstead, then shrugged. It would do for one night. Tomorrow he'd go back up to the ranch; maybe stake out where the buildings were going to be; maybe go fishing in Roan's Creek; just lie there in the grass with memories washing over him.

He sat on the edge of the bed and levered off his boots. It was good to be back; it was good to feel like you belonged somewhere.

CHAPTER TWO

He remembered his parents talking of Maine, where they came from, a vague and distant place girded with rocks and bound by hard winters. Thinking back sometimes, was pleasant in a painful way, and the sum of recollection inclined him to believe his parents had settled the emerald meadows because they reminded them of Maine. Small, rich fields interspersed with fingerlings of forest, along the swift-falling curves and bends of the watershed they had called Roan's Creek.

It was easy to recall the slab-house under trees that leaned and creaked like antiquated gladiators when winter hurled its fierce assaults. And the creek that flowed southward, down towards the flat belly of prairie, and squandered its clear-water strength there. And the crooked road wrought by his father with its fringe of shade the full length; a narrow old snake of a road, all shade-mottled and dusty looking, leading up out of the prairie into the blue-shaggy Beyond; into the highland where deer and bear and all manner of game lived; where meadows lay hidden, swollen with stirrup-high grass.

There was a great fullness to the uplands, where the land swept back from the prairie-desert, broadening out, lifting higher and becoming wilder in its rich fertility until it burst against the sky in a dark and straining way.

Somehow, Ben thought, and not only because there was beauty up there, that land had a hold on him. He'd travelled far and wide, seen tons of country, some full of beauty and a grand solemnity that made a man hurt for looking on it; some harsh and forbidding, some jagged and untamed, or tilted against the flaming sunsets, or flat and docile, but he had never seen a country that reached down inside and gripped him like the uplands he'd known since infancy, held him now.

He *belonged* there. Nothing; man, animal, or element, could turn him away. Least of all the Marlows. He arose and dressed with these thoughts; he ate at the diner with them for company, then he went over and bought a sturdy wagon from the liveryman, to implement them. He also bought a team of big bay horses, a good set of harness. Then he drove to the Deming Mercantile Company and loaded up kegs of nails, a big grindstone, two axes and two saws, all the impedimenta of building, all the requisites for putting down roots. And finally, with his saddlehorse tied to the tailgate, his carbine on the seat beside him, he took his way northward out of Deming.

Cliff Thompson lingered in the shade of the Oases Saloon's overhang, smoking a cigarette, and watching. When the wagon was lost in the shimmering, heat-scourged distance, he flung the cigarette down and stamped on it. It irritated him that Ben Roan would not see that he was heading straight for a killing; his own or someone else's.

" 'Morning, Marshal. Wasn't that Ben Roan that drove that wagon out of town?"

Thompson bent a hard look at the lawyer. "It was," he said shortly. "Why didn't you tell him to wait until there was a hearing over that road before going up there?"

"Someone has to bring action before there's any case, Marshal."

Thompson looked unpleasant. "Yeh," he said. "I know. There are two sides to the law — your side and my side. I get paid to prevent trouble and you get paid for starting it. In fact, you don't get paid unless it *does* start."

Charley Bell squinted northward. "Unless there's a restraining order issued to prevent him from using that road, it's his right to use it. He can go up there any time he wants to. You know that. So far there's been only talk, and talk doesn't mean a thing."

"Law-book theory," Thompson said shortly. "Did you ever try law-book theory against a cocked pistol, Bell?"

"Don't be ridiculous. As a matter of fact, you should be riding up there with him. That's the only way you can prevent trouble — stop it before it starts. If you can do that, there'll be no need for attorneys."

"Now who's being ridiculous? You know damned well I can't forbid either the Marlows or Ben Roan from fighting one another without a court order, and by the time I get the order, the killing has already begun. I wish folks who make laws had to carry law books in their holsters instead of guns."

Bell continued to squint into the distance and Marshal Thompson fell into a deep and disgusted silence. A solitary vertical groove of disapproval lay deep between his eyebrows.

Ben drove steadily and did not look back. Deming squatted far back in the quivering heat one moment, and the next moment it blurred into a soiled murk low against the roll of far horizon. His thoughts were on other things. The Marlows might have money now, good horses and a large herd, but he knew men; that kind didn't change inwardly. He knew from a dozen gunfights that it was what lay inside men that counted, not their bankrolls nor their herds, nor the quality of their stock. The Marlows had never had it, and all the money in the world wouldn't put it into them.

They might try scaring him out; probably would. Or they might shoot his horses, or even try to bushwhack him, but when it came to stand-up-and-fight, or cut and run, lead bullets or fast horses, he knew which way they'd go.

He forged steadily ahead towards the blue-shadows where the land swelled upwards with a heavy lift and fullness. He kept a sharp watch but made no attempt to conceal his coming by clinging to the creek-willows or the meagre shadows. If they were watching, let them watch. If they'd found a pinch of guttiness among them, let them show it.

He was drinking in the beauty of the shade and the uplands' deep silence when movement to his right, a quiver of colour, of red and white, snagged at the corner of his vision. Facing swiftly half around, one hand moving in a blur, he saw the horse, head up, tail high and waving, running westward. A lemon-yellow sun, burning-huge, cast a haziness over the distance. He watched the horse long enough to discern flopping stirrups and broken reins, then he back-tracked with his eyes to where the sprawl of colour lay in the dead grass; swung the team, urged them closer and kept staring at the vivid hues until he was close enough to make out arms and legs, then he slowed, set the brake and jumped down.

He rolled her over with one hand, straightened her limbs and knelt there wondering who she was, where she had come from. Her blouse was tight-rising, violent red, and her riding skirt was creamy and expensive looking. Her face, even in unconsciousness, was square, full-lipped, and wilful appearing, and a thick riot of auburn hair glistened fiercely in the sunlight. He shaded her face with his hat and waited. She was uninjured so far as he could see, except for being knocked senseless by the fall. He twisted to look after the horse. It had disappeared.

He was smoking and studying the upland shadows when she said, "Oh . . . !" He punched out the cigarette, lifted her head and smoothed away the hair.

"What happened, ma'm?"

"Oh . . . He bucked me off."

He propped her against his knee, put his hat back on and bent to shield her from the sun. "Nothing's broken that I could find."

The girl felt the back of her head and said, "Ouch!"

He watched her a moment, then gripped her by both arms. "Come on; you can stand up. I'll drive you home."

She looked into his face for the first time, and her long eyes narrowed. "Who are you?"

"Ben Roan. I own some land up in the foothills."

"Roan . . . ?" She blinked and stared.

He nodded. "And who are you, ma'm?"

"Sarahlee Marlow."

He stared. "Marlow? Kin to old Will and the others?"

"Will is my uncle. The boys are my cousins."

"I don't recollect ever hearing of any other Marlows hereabouts."

"My people live in Santa Fe. I've been up here since last May looking after grandpaw. He's very old."

"Well," Ben said, helping her to arise. "Come on; I'll drive you on up to the Marlow place."

While he was setting the lines straight with his back to her, she straightened her clothes, brushed herself off, and looked westerly, after the horse, with anger in her eyes, but she said nothing. He helped her up, went around and climbed up beside her, and flicked the lines. The team leaned, the wagon ground back onto the road, and for a while the only sound was of iron tyres grinding down into the gritty dust.

Where the green bog lay the ascent began. Ben slapped with the lines, the team leaned into their collars, and the trail steepened. Not until they were on the level again, moving through tree-shade, did the girl speak.

"What you're doing is foolish, Mr. Roan."

"Is it?" Ben said easily, without looking around at her. "It doesn't seem that way to me." He let the lines lie slack. The team dropped their heads and toed into the next upgrade.

"My cousins won't let you do it."

He turned, finally, and gazed at her. "You know, ma'm, I've heard that before. I didn't believe it then, and I don't believe it now."

"You have no right-of-way to the old Roan place."

"Ma'm, my father built this road almost thirty years ago. Before the Marlows were in this country."

"But the road hasn't been used since you left."

"Maybe not, but whether I've got a right or not is for a law-court to decide — not your cousins, or your uncle." Ben shrugged slightly, studied the land ahead, then said, "I can't make old Will like the idea of my being up in here, but he might as well get used to the idea."

She studied his profile for a moment, before she said, "You're going to make a lot of unnecessary trouble, Mr. Roan."

"No; I'm not going to make any trouble. All I'm going to do is build a cabin, a barn, some corrals, and try to live in peace. If there's trouble it won't be me that starts it." He was going to say more when movement among the trees ahead caught his attention. The lines lay in his left hand; the right hand was curled and moving when a big-framed man moved out into the road in front of the team. He was holding a carbine one-handed; it was cocked.

"That's far enough, Roan."

Ben recognised Harold Marlow. "Hello, Hal," he said quietly.

"Sarahlee!" The way Marlow said it, it sounded like 'Sally'. "What'n tarnation you doing up there?"

"That horse El gave me bucked me off."

41

"Are you hurt?"

"No; but ——"

"El told you he was green-broke. It's a wonder you didn't get hurt bad." Marlow gestured with the carbine. "Get down off'n there."

"Wait a minute," Ben said. "She'll get down when you empty that carbine."

The big man looked hard at Roan. "Empty hell," he said. "You're not talking to Guy now. You're going to turn that caravan around and head back out of here."

" 'Be a shame to see you kill your cousin," Ben said. "Be sure you shoot straight, Hal."

"Roan! Don't try it!"

"Behind two big horses and beside a girl? Of course I'm going to try it. The odds're in my favour."

One of the team-horses blew its nose and the girl started. Her single *"Don't!"* was half scream, half sob. Neither man looked at her. The silence was tight around them all. "Harold, let him go."

"Can't, Sarahlee; you know that."

"Then wait until I get down."

Ben caught her right wrist with his left hand. He never took his eyes off Hal. "All right," he said. "Drop it or shoot it!"

"No, Harold — please NO!"

Marlow stood like stone, his eyes dark

with indecision, then the carbine barrel began to dip. His face was grey, his lips sucked flat and bloodless.

"All the way, Hal."

The gun made a small rustling sound as it fell into the dust.

"Now the shell-belt."

When Marlow was disarmed Ben relaxed his grip on the girl's wrist, thrust the lines into her hands and pointed ahead with his pistol barrel. "Drive, ma'm," he said sharply, and as the wagon started past Marlow, Ben twisted on the seat, watching him. As long as he was in sight, Hal Marlow stood there in the road, as motionless as stone, outrage in every line. When the wagon was cresting the last rise and drop-off, Ben holstered his gun and swivelled back around on the seat. Without looking at the hot-eyed girl he pointed to the creek-crossing.

"Make for that little ford over there by the cottonwoods," he said.

Beyond lay the shady clearing where the house had been. Ben got down near an old apple tree, began to unharness the team, and ignored Sarahlee Marlow until she said, "I suppose I can walk back now."

He flung the harness over a tree-limb, pushed back his hat and faced around. "If you like," he said. "But for your help the

43

least I could do is make some supper and take you back a-horseback."

She regarded him steadily for a moment before spitting out the words: "Hiding behind my skirts!"

He smiled thinly. "Not your skirts, ma'm — behind the team."

"You used me!"

He went to the back of the wagon, got a bucket, crossed over and held it towards her. "Get some water from the creek. I'll peel some potatoes. After we eat I'll take you back."

"They'll kill you."

"Maybe," he looked pointedly at the bucket, "but not on an empty stomach anyway. Go on."

She got the water and returned with it, set it beside him and stood there ramrod-straight. He worked up a cooking-fire without speaking, and when the food was cooking he stood up. "Watch it," he said, "while I care for the horses."

When he returned from hobbling the animals he had washed at the creek, she was conscious of his nearness but neither looked around nor spoke. He made two chairs and a table with wooden boxes, laid out two tin plates and eating hardware, then sat back making a cigarette, watching her.

"How's your head?"

"Even with the bump, it's got more sense in it than yours has."

He lit up and exhaled, reached for a plate and said, "You must be feeling all right. Those potatoes look good." He tried them and looked over at her. "Are you always so skittery?"

"What do you mean?"

"You were scared stiff back there."

She flushed angrily. "Two fools with guns and me in the middle — why wouldn't I be?"

"Neither one of us was going to shoot."

She sat back and ate a moment before replying. She was clearly struggling to master her indignation. "Mr. Roan, do you honestly believe my cousins won't kill you?"

"Yes'm. I honestly believe they won't."

"But — why? They live less than four miles from here. You *know* how they feel about you being up here. You *should* know by now . . ."

"I just don't believe coyotes can become wolves, ma'm. I've known my share of both and I've yet to see either of 'em change."

She gazed at him steadily. "Do you think my cousins are cowards?"

"Not cowards — cautious men. Twice now they've dry-gulched me, and both times they've backed down, even with the drop."

"But ——"

"No buts, ma'm. A man who is going to kill, does it. He doesn't talk about it — wave guns around. I've known those Marlows a long time. You aren't the first person who's told me how tough they are — but I remember how they used to be, and nothing'll change the spots on a man — not even success."

She put her plate aside and said almost the same thing Cliff Thompson had said, "You're very stubborn, Mr. Roan. *I* know my cousins and uncle better than you do, and *I* say they *will* kill you."

"They may try. I won't deny that. Bushwhacking seems to run in your family. That's the only way they'll kill me."

She stood up and said, "You're impossible," then she gathered up the plates and started for the creek with them. He watched her kneel and scrub the utensils with sand, and smiled to himself. Then he went over and began unloading the wagon. When she returned, placed the cleansed pans and plates face-down on the boxes, he caught his saddle horse and bridled him. She walked over near him and said, "You're blind, Mr. Roan. Conceitedly blind."

"Well now, I've been called lots of things,

but never conceited before. Look, ma'm, men who fight don't run to lawyers, they run for guns. Your uncle's got a lawyer down in Deming. He's going to try and close the road by law. I can understand him not wanting anyone to run cattle up here; it's always been good stock country. But he isn't going to kill anyone to keep it like that."

"What's to stop El and Hal from killing you, then?"

"Me."

"That's conceit, Mr. Roan," Sarahlee said. "Why, you could have been killed a few minutes ago, while you were eating supper."

"Nope; you were my protection. Not even a Marlow would risk a drygulch like that."

"And tomorrow night?"

He slapped the latigo tight, lowered the stirrup and turned towards her. "I've seen men bushwhacked," he said. "It won't be that easy for them."

"You're hopeless."

He mounted, swung the horse close, kicked his left leg forward and waited. She toed into the stirrup and swung up behind the cantle. As the horse moved out into the opening by the creek, she said, "Not down the road. Over by that deadfall there's a deer trail that'll take us down in back of my uncle's house."

"You've been up here before?"

"Often, yes."

Neither of them spoke again until the road through the trees widened into a clearing where racked-up firewood was curing, then Sarahlee said, "Don't go any closer. I can walk from here."

He stopped, kicked his foot free of the stirrup and she got down. In the gloom of dusk she looked up at him briefly, then turned abruptly and disappeared among the trees. He sat motionless for sixty seconds listening to the whip and snap of underbrush, then he turned back.

The next morning he was stirring before sunup. He felled cedars, snaked them in with the team, set them on stones for mudsills, and worked without respite until late in the afternoon, then he cared for the horses, dragged his bedding back into the trees, and slept like the dead. This routine engrossed him for six days, and finally, with the walls and roof of the cabin finished, he gave way to the puzzlement which had been growing with the days. He had never once relaxed vigilance; the horses were his sentinels, but not once had they thrown up their heads at other than the normal scents and sights. He laid aside his tools, washed at the creek, ate, then made a wide, swinging circuit around the meadow — and found no tracks at all. On the seventh day, when he was nailing shakes on the roof, the horses finally warned him by freezing into statues, their heads pointing south. He slid off the roof, stepped into the evening dusk where his carbine stood, and waited.

"Halloo . . ."

"Who is it? Ride up closer and keep your hands in plain sight."

"It's me — Thompson."

"Ride on in."

The marshal reined up near the cabin. "Satisfied?" he asked, with a frown.

"Glad to see you. Get down; there's a ring in that tree behind you, tie your horse there." While Thompson was caring for his mount, Ben entered the cabin, put up his carbine and poked up a fire in the Cannon stove, swished the coffee pot and put it over a burner. When the marshal blocked the doorway he said, "Come on in. Coffee'll be hot in a minute."

"Darker'n the inside of a well in here."

"I eat by the setting sun," Ben said, moving around the room letting rolled-up blanket-blinds fall over the openings. "Don't use lanterns very often." When the room was totally dark he felt his way to the lamp, lit it, and looked into the marshal's pinched-down eyes.

Thompson looked around slowly, at the walls and ceiling, the carefully wrought cupboards, the pine-scented table and four chairs. He shook his head gently. "You sure been busy," he said, pulling back a chair and dropping down. "I brought a shovel along to bury you."

Ben took up a towel and headed for the door. "You're either too early for that, or too late, I'm not sure which. Pour us some coffee while I sluice off at the creek." When he returned to the cabin, Thompson had tossed his hat on the table and poured the coffee. He sipped his slowly and watched Ben comb his hair, cross to the table and drop down.

"Had any visitors, Roan?"

"Not a one. I can't understand it. I thought sure that they'd have tried to bushwhack me by now."

Thompson looked around the room again. "I didn't know you had it in you, Roan. Cupboards, too, an' chairs."

"I've done a few odd jobs in my time, Marshal. I'll tell you one thing, you sure sleep nights after doing this all day. But it's worth it."

"Is it?"

"Is it what?"

"Worth it." Thompson put his cup down and gazed across the table at Ben. "Haven't you wondered why they haven't tried to chouse you out of here?"

"I wondered."

"Here," the marshal said, holding out a paper. "Read it."

"What is it?"

"A court order for me to evict you until there's a hearing on whether you can use the road or not."

"Hell; I'm not using the road."

"But you did use it, and you'll use it again. By the way, did you get the title transferred to your name?"

"I did." Ben studied the court order briefly then tossed it onto the table. "You mean to tell me I can't live on my own land because I used that damned road to get up here?"

"Nothing's been said about what you did *after* you used the road. All that paper says is that you can't stay up here until the right-of-way's been adjudicated. And *I'm* not telling you anything; the court is."

Ben lowered his head, worked up a cigarette, lit it and gazed at Marshal Thompson. "You know," he said softly, "I'm beginning to get tired of this game."

"I tried to get you to stay in town until

there was a hearing — don't blame me."

"I'm not blaming you, Marshal. Maybe I ought to blame myself for ever coming back here."

The lawman slapped his leg and stood up. "Just one thing more: don't start anything. Don't go hunting them, and don't go ridin' near any clumps of brush or blind arroyos. Let the court decide who's right and who's wrong, and meanwhile, get a room in Deming." Thompson looked at Roan a moment, then dumped his hat on the back of his head and said, "Why don't you ride back with me tonight?"

"How long have I got to vacate?"

"Tomorrow at high noon. But what's the sense of stayin'? Throw some stuff in your saddlebags and I'll catch your horse." The marshal started towards the blanket-draped doorway. "Are the work-horses branded?"

"Hoof-branded."

"That's good enough."

Ben stood up with a nod. "I reckon. All right; I'll gather up some duds and be right out."

By the time Ben blew out the lantern, Marshal Thompson had his horse caught, saddled and bridled. He stood hip-shot while Ben fastened the saddlebags aft of the cantle, then they both mounted. Ben led

out. Their passing left hollow echoes, especially when they clattered across the creek.
For two miles they rode stirrup, neither saying much, then, just above the last rise, and
near a curve in the trail, a horseman
emerged from the shadows and Ben heard
Cliff Thompson suck in his breath as he was
going off the far side of his mount. He had
the animal swung against his body, his gun
cocked and rising, when the marshal's
voice, harsh and stabbing, broke the hush.

"This is U.S. Marshal Thompson from —"

"*Sarahlee!*"

Thompson looked around and down. Ben
moved around the horse and forward.
Moonlight glinted from the gun in his fist.

"You've got a knack of getting between
men and guns, haven't you? What're you
doing up here this time of night?"

"Waiting for you," she said, and looked at
Cliff Thompson. "Would you ride on, Marshal? Mr. Roan will catch up with you."

Thompson peered curiously at the girl,
then nudged his horse on past. As soon as
he was gone Sarahlee slid off her horse. Ben
watched her come closer. Pale moonlight
flooded around them, frogs called huskily
to one another, and a boomer-hawk
rumbled once and was gone. When she
stopped, gazing at him and saying nothing,

he looked past her, and at the black shadows on both sides of the road, then he said, "Well, what're they waiting for? Have to draw straws to see who takes the first shot?"

Her face froze and anger flamed out at him. "I guess they were right after all. You're just too conceited. I rode up here to see you — to warn you . . . It was a waste of time." She turned, snatched at the reins and his voice halted her.

"Hold it; what'd you expect me to think; somebody coming out in the trail like that? I've been expecting a shot for a week now."

"Well, go on expecting it. You're going to get it. Don't think you aren't." She mounted. He moved swiftly forward, grabbed the cheek-piece of her bridle and held on.

"All right. I'm not going to run from it. When? When do I get it? That's what you came up here to tell me, isn't it?"

"Yes."

"I'm listening."

"They've sent for a gunman. He's to hunt you up in Deming."

"What's his name and when's he coming?"

"I don't know. I only know they sent for him. I heard my uncle and Hal talking about it. As soon as I came up they changed the subject, but I'd heard. I was feeding the chickens behind the barn. They said it would be best for him to kill you in Deming, after you'd been served the eviction notice; that way no one would connect your killing with us — with them." She looked down at him a moment. "They said you cost them a lot of money; that the gunman had to be imported from Wyoming. Why didn't you tell me you were *the* Ben Roan?"

"You didn't ask," he said flatly. "Why did you tell me this?"

She tossed her head and the auburn hair glinted copper in the moonlight. "You deserve a chance, don't you?"

"Even a dog deserves that."

"Is that the only reason?"

"Yes. Now let go of my bridle."

He did. She whirled the horse and rode off through the trees without a backward glance. He stood there listening, then he went to his own mount, vaulted into the saddle, and spurred after Marshal Thompson, who was smoking placidly by the seepage spring a half mile farther along. When Ben reined up Thompson mounted without a word, and they continued on down the trail side by side.

Not until they were within sight of Deming did Cliff Thompson clear his throat, and say, "You know, Roan, you look like just an average feller to me. There's something about you I can't figure out, though. That big girl back there — that Sarahlee Marlow. Half the riders in the country been trying all summer to take her to the socials, and she won't go with any of them. You come along, roil up her kinsmen, and she stays up half the night to warn you about a hired killer."

Ben looked sharply at Thompson. "You snuck back, didn't you?"

"Yes," the marshal admitted candidly. "My job's to prevent trouble. If that was bait for a drygulch, I wanted to stop it. Anyway, Sarahlee warns you against her own kinsmen, and that's downright unusual — especially for a Marlow. They're usually as clanny as a pack of wolves." Thompson looked around. "But that's only half of it. For the past week Bedelia's been asking me about you 'most every day."

"Bedelia?"

"Yeah. Your lawyer's daughter."

"Oh, Della."

"Della then. Now, what I can't figure out is what a feller like you's got that makes two girls like that all a-flutter about you."

Ben swung across the roadway towards the liverybarn and dismounted. When the hostler came up he handed him his reins and waited for the marshal to get down, then he said, "Most folks feel sorry for an underdog, Marshal. Maybe that's it."

As he was walking across the roadway the marshal looked after him in disgust. "Underdog! Yeah — I'm sure that's it. Good night, Hank."

"Good night, Marshal. Say, ain't that Ben Roan you come in with?"

"It was."

"Is he wanted?"

"Well, not by me, Hank — not yet anyway."

"You know, I got a cousin over at Wagon Mount told me one time, when Roan was shotgun for Wells Fargo, that he ——"

"Good *night,* Hank!"

CHAPTER THREE

Ben saw Charley Bell at his office the following morning. Handed him the vacating order and slouched in a chair while Bell read it.

"At least they're doing it legally," Bell said. Roan's blue eyes rested on Bell's face for a moment, but he said nothing. "There are two things we can do, Mr. Roan. We can appeal for temporary permission on the grounds that you live up there; that you need temporary access pending the court's decision; or we can abide by this order and wait until the twentieth, when the case will be heard, which is eleven days from now."

Eleven days. Ben looked out the window into the shimmering roadway. On one of those eleven days a stranger would ride into Deming. He moved in the chair. Eleven days of watching; of keeping his back to walls; of living a lifetime in less than two weeks. He got up and said, "I'll wait."

"I'd advise that, Mr. Roan. Eleven days isn't a long time."

"No?" The cold stare made Bell uncomfortable. "It can be forever, Mr. Bell."

The lawyer looked at Ben inquiringly, but Roan did not elaborate, so he said, "This has become a *cause célèbre* in Deming, which is unusual. Ordinarily gunfights draw attention, not legal battles."

"You don't think this will end in a gunfight?"

Bell smoothed the papers before him with both hands and did not look at Ben when he replied, "I don't believe it *should,* Mr. Roan. Another thing — I remembered where I'd heard your name before. I was in Raton last summer and —"

"I was there, too. There was a fight with a cowboy from Las Crucas . . ."

"Yes."

"Forget it," Ben said shortly. "If you want me I'll be around the Oases Hotel."

He returned to the glittering sunlight outside, and a man who was shuffling past paused, looked around, then stopped. It was the blacksmith.

" 'Heard the Marlows got you put off, Ben. 'That right?"

"I guess you could say that, Joel. It amounts to an eleven-day waiting period, until the court sits."

"An' what if they decide against you?"

Ben saw Marshal Thompson come out of the abstract office and start south towards his office. "Why then," he replied to Partin disinterestedly, "I reckon I'll have to sprout wings and fly in there, Joel."

Partin made a polite smile. "I don't know much about the law," he said, "but I know this much; if them Marlows got a mind to, they can keep dragging you into court from now 'til doomsday. There'll always be law-yers willing to take their money."

"That's one way to fight, all right," Ben said, watching the marshal disappear into his office. "But y'know, Joel, I got a notion this'll be over before the eleven days are up."

"What eleven days?" Partin asked eagerly.

"The eleven days between now and when the court sits, on the twentieth."

Partin's eyes lingered on Ben's face a moment, then he mumbled something, stepped down off the walkway and strode angrily towards his shop. Ben watched him go with a faint smile; Joel Partin was a regular magpie of a man; he carried everything he heard to Cliff Thompson.

Later in the day, feeling restless and futile, Ben drifted down to the liverybarn. The place was cool and strong with an ammonia scent. A few old men sat on a bench just inside the doorway, talking desultorily, and whittling. They scarcely looked up when he entered. He leaned on the door of his horse's stall and gazed at the animal. It had been curried, grained, and there was a bait of timothy hay in the manger. He drifted back outside, studied the town a while, then drifted over to the Oases Saloon.

Three of the eleven days went by like that, with nothing to do, with time hanging hot and still, then, on the fourth day, as he was coming out of the Deming Mercantile Company's store with an unopened sack of tobacco in his hands, he came face to face with Bedelia Bell. Her face looked flushed from the heat and her eyes shone with quick recognition. He inclined his head and said, "Good morning, ma'm."

"Good morning, Mr. Roan. Paw told me what happened. I think it's a shame, what the Marlows are trying to do."

A twinkle appeared in his gaze. "You know, I do too," he said.

She smiled and colour darkened her face. "You're making fun of me. Paw says the hearing will be on the twentieth, when the circuit judge gets here."

"If there is a hearing."

Her smile vanished and she looked closely

at him. "What do you mean by that?"

"The twentieth's a week off, ma'm. That's a long time in some ways. Anything could happen between now and then."

Her glance wavered and the colour receded. Something he had not seen before crossed her face, a sharp inquisitiveness. With significant emphasis she said, "I hope nothing happens, Mr. Roan. Nothing that's illegal."

His eyebrows went up. Beneath them, his glance was sardonic. "Illegal, ma'm? Why, I don't usually do illegal things. But I sure have no qualms about killing to stay alive, either."

"Are you saying you think the Marlows may try to kill you?"

He shook his head at her, touched his hat and moved off. Across the road Marshal Thompson was watching him from beneath the overhang in front of the abstract office. When Ben crossed the roadway, Thompson flipped away his cigarette, pushed off the wall and nodded. Ben fell in beside him and they started north towards the liverybarn.

"She's just about the prettiest thing I ever saw, Roan."

"Yeah," Ben said thoughtfully. "Marshal, 'you know the difference between a pretty woman and a pretty horse?"

"Of course I do."

"Do you? When you buy a pretty horse and it turns out to be nothing but pretty, you can sell it. When you marry a pretty woman and *she* turns out to be nothing but pretty — you're stuck for the rest of your life."

Thompson looked around. "Is that what you think of Della Bell?"

Ben squinted at the lawman innocently. "I was talking about horses," he said. "Say, a peddler came into the liverybarn while I was down there a while ago. He had some watermelons with him. I'll split one with you."

They bought a melon, took it out back in the shade and cut it open. Ben ate his half standing up, leaning against the barn. Thompson found a rickety nail keg and used it for a chair.

" 'Think there's going to be a fight, don't you?" the marshal said, juice running down his chin.

Ben half-smiled. "Good old Joel," he said. "What would you do without him, Marshal?"

"You sure got it in for Joel, haven't you?"

"No. He's like looking through a window. Everything you want spread around you hang up in front of him. Sure; I think there's going to be a fight. In fact, I know there is."

"Let me tell you something about Joel," the marshal said, spitting seeds against the ground. "Riders crossing the desert from the west cover a lot of rocky country."

"What of it?"

"When they hit Deming they head straight for the blacksmith's shop for new shoes on their animals. Now this morning, for example, a feller rode in, left his horse to be shod, and while he was over at the Oases Joel got curious."

"That curiosity'll get him shot some day." Ben threw aside a rind and reached for more melon. "What'd he do — go through the feller's saddlebags?"

"Yep."

"The dirty ——"

"Hold it. I'm not through. This stranger had two wanted posters with his pictures on 'em, folded up in a piece of oilskin."

Ben held the watermelon without biting into it. He was watching Thompson. "Well, what about them?"

"Joel kept one poster and put the other one back."

"He brought you the one he kept?"

"Right again. I looked through my files but found nothing. Of course, that's nothing unusual, especially since this feller's from Wyoming, not New Mexico."

"So you arrested him."

Thompson wiped his chin with a sleeve and reached for more melon. "Nope. I meant to, but when I got down to Joel's he was gone."

"And here you sit eating watermelon."

"I sent telegrams to every town around, and I put out two posses." The marshal looked at Ben quizzically. "I learned long ago the best way to catch these fellers is to stay close to the telegraph office in town, and put out posses. Sort of like a general directs his armies."

Ben ate his watermelon in silence, wiped his hands and face on a handkerchief, and said, "Five more days."

"What? What're you talking about?" Before Ben could answer Thompson's face cleared. "Oh," he said. "The twentieth — the trial. Yeah; five more days. We were talking about Joel Partin, remember?"

"I remember. I do a lot of remembering."

"Well, thanks for the melon. I got to get back to the telegraph office."

Ben went to his room over the Oases, locked the door, placed a chair against it, sat on the edge of the bed facing the opened window, and cleaned his six-gun. Five more days to go. 'Be a shame if the Marlows had to pay the hired gun, and a lawyer too.

He rubbed the holster down until it shone, dropped the pistol into it and drew it; did that many times, then propped himself up on the bed and gazed out where the sun was going down; out where heat-haze made the world dance and glitter. A man could tolerate a lot, he thought, so long as he is moving; it's the standing still, the waiting, that ties him in knots inwardly.

He watched two little boys teasing a girl with pigtails, down, and across, the road. The little girl's back was as straight as a ramrod; she tried to ignore her tormentors; then she turned swiftly and swung at them with little-girl awkwardness. The boys, never dreaming she would strike at them, were caught unprepared; one fell, more because he tripped over a loose board in the plank-walk than because the little girl's blow was well aimed. The other boy backed away, then he doubled over laughing, and even Ben Roan's face had a ghost of a smile on it. The little girl turned and ran. A buggy flashing past with dusty yellow wheels hid her from the man at the window. He looked at the driver and was jolted out of his reverie. Sarahlee Marlow.

His boots struck the floor as he arose, took up his hat and left the room. By the time he was down on the plankwalk the yellow-wheeled rig was standing empty in front of the mercantile store. He studied the town with deliberate care for a moment, then started towards the buggy. The sun was lowering rapidly; long, splintery shadows were coming out.

There weren't many people at the mercantile establishment. None he recognised, and only a few who looked at him as he went past, approaching Sarahlee from the rear. "Evening, ma'm." When she turned he saw the anxiety in her face at once. "I owe you a dinner. I'd like to pay the debt right now, if you've got the time."

"No," she said, hesitantly. "Wait a minute." The clerk held out a small bag. She took it, paid him, and faced back around. "Take a drive with me, Mr. Roan."

"My pleasure, ma'm."

He handed her into the rig, got in on the left side, eased off the foot-brake and took up the lines. "Any particular place?"

"Out of town," she said.

From the corner of his eye he saw how erect she sat. How her eyes flicked over the people they passed. He guessed the reason for her agitation with no trouble, and decided to remain quiet until she relaxed.

When they were well away from town, with dusk fast settling, she leaned back and let out a long breath. Where a pale lift of land stood aloof and lonely, Ben came upon a buggy parked beneath some scraggly oaks. With a twinkle in his eyes he said, "I've noticed that run-about in Deming. 'Belongs to a young buck who dresses like a real dude."

"Young fellow?"

"Maybe twenty, twenty-one."

"You don't have to drive so close," she said in a low voice, and after he'd swung wide, she looked up. "Is he younger than you are, Mr. Roan?"

"I'd say about a hundred years younger, ma'm." He looked at her. "I'm twenty-five."

"That's not old."

"It depends on how you use the years."

"How old do you think I am?"

He continued to gaze at her. The pale light made her skin like velvet. Her mouth was heavy, her eyes wide and long. There was a sprinkle of girlhood's freckles across the saddle of her nose.

"Well . . . ?"

"Nineteen. I guessed that once before — the day that horse dumped you."

"I'm twenty." She pointed with an out-flung arm. "See that fringe of sage over there? Drive over that way. There's an old Indian camp-ground there."

He obeyed, and tied up at a big oak tree, helped her down and walked through the benign, still night at her side. When she stopped and turned to face him, he could hear his heart sloshing, loud as distant thunder, and wondered if she heard it, too.

"Has the gunman come?" she asked.

"Maybe; I'm not sure. A stranger rode in this morning. A Wyoming stranger."

"Do you know his name?"

"No."

"I do; it's Rockwell. He rides a leggy sorrel horse, is about your height, and wears an ivory-handled gun."

"I didn't see him myself, I just heard about him."

"That's why I came to town today," Sarahlee said. "Well, I needed some thread, too." She turned away from him. "He came by the ranch this morning early. I got a good look at him."

"How do you know he's the same man?"

"Uncle Will talked to him. They stood out in the middle of the yard where no one could get close to them. Uncle Will handed him some money."

"Could've been a cattle buyer," Ben said, not believing it.

Sarahlee whirled. "There's just one thing worse than stubbornness," she said swiftly.

"That's conceit."

"All right. His name's Rockwell, he has an ivory-butted gun, and he rides a sorrel horse. I believe you; I'll keep my eyes skinned for him. And . . . I'm grateful, ma'm."

"You don't have to be," she said, turning away again. "I'm doing this to keep my uncle out of trouble — that's all."

He stood there looking at the sky, and after a time he said, "The moon'll be full tomorrow night, ma'm."

Her shoulders stiffened and she neither turned nor spoke.

"You know, this country may be hell on horses and women, like they say, but I'll bet Paradise is no prettier of a summer evening."

"You may find out before long."

Without looking down he said, "I may, and then again I may not."

"I've heard how fast you are."

"Have you? You must think I'm awful slow right this minute."

That brought her around with pinpoints of flame in her glance. "What did you mean by that?"

He lowered his eyes to her face, stood there in the soft-scented night looking at her. He sighed. "I never felt so detached before; it's kind of like I'm looking down from atop a mountain somewhere."

"That's very poor poetry, Mr. Roan."

"I expect it is, but it's the only way I know to say what I'm thinking."

She bit her lip. "I'm sorry; I didn't mean that."

"It doesn't matter, ma'm. Well, I expect we'd better be getting back. Your folks'll be wondering what's keeping you so long in Deming."

She walked behind him to the buggy, got in without waiting to be assisted, settled back as he got in, swung the horse, and let it pick its way back towards town. She watched him make a cigarette and smoke it in total silence. Just before they entered Deming she put a hand lightly on his arm. "I didn't mean to get angry back there, Mr. Roan."

He looked at her from a calm face. "Did you get mad back there?" he asked softly. "I didn't notice."

He got down near the Oases, thanked her again and stood in the gloom watching the rig disappear northward. A voice from the shadows came softly towards him.

"I been waiting two hours for you to get back."

Ben turned. "Evening, Marshal."

Thompson loomed up, stopped, and looked after the buggy for a while before speaking. "Y'know, I'm not exactly the marrying type, but I've often thought if I was, I'd sure give that filly a run for her money."

"You've been waiting two hours to tell me that?"

Thompson shook his head. "No, not exactly. I been waiting to tell you that Wyoming gun-hand disappeared."

"Why tell me?"

The marshal faced around and leaned upon an overhang upright. "When we were eating that melon, this afternoon, I got the definite impression you were interested in him. In fact, you never finished your half of the melon. I got to pondering about that — and one thing and another — like that girl warning you the other night. 'You want to know what I came up with?"

"It might be interesting, at that, Marshal."

"That someone's out to kill you, and you know it."

"Like who; the Wyoming gun-hand?"

"Maybe. Does the name Jake Rockwell mean anything to you?"

"Should it? Is that the Wyoming feller's handle?"

"It is. Listen, Ben; I know your reputation. I also know my job pretty well. Maybe you want to settle this your way. Well, ordinarily, that'd be fine with me. But as it happens I get paid for keeping the peace around here."

"As far as I know," Ben replied quietly, "No one's broken the peace."

"Not yet, you mean."

"All right, not yet. Marshal, if someone's out to down me, I'll be around for him to find. I don't start many fights and I don't run from many, either. And while we're jawing let me get something else off my chest. I know what the Marlows're up to. They started this and they're going to be in at the finish. You know cussed well I've done everything but bend over backwards to avoid trouble. I can't spend the rest of my life being like that — no man could."

"All I'm saying, Ben, is that if you know something's going to happen, it's your duty to let me know first."

"What good would that do?"

"Well, you take Rockwell. I'll lock him up just as soon's the boys find him, and that'll be the end of that."

Ben shook his head. "You know better than that. You lock Rockwell up — there'll be another one. You lock up the next one — there'll be still another one. That's the way this killing business goes and you know it."

"All I know," Thompson said flatly, "is that I don't want any trouble."

"Who does? I sure don't. I just want to build my place back there in the foothills. But listen, Marshal; I've got some help with this Rockwell feller. Maybe I won't get any help with the next bushwhacker. I don't aim to wait and find out, because sooner or later one of these gunhands'll catch me off-guard."

Thompson studied the darkened roadway a moment, then he straightened up off the post and thrust fisted hands deep into his trouser pockets. "You're talking like a man who means to carry his private war into the enemy's camp, Ben."

"That's exactly what I aim to do — after I meet Rockwell. That's the only sensible way I know to settle this damned business once and for all."

"In a few more days the circuit judge'll be here and he'll settle things."

"No he won't. He'll settle the road business, but he won't settle this business of hired guns. There's only one way to settle that."

Thompson squinted at the moon. "It's getting late," he said, resignedly. "I reckon I'll turn in. Just remember, Ben, the first shot brings me on the run."

"I'll remember. I may even fire it myself, to get some help."

Marshal Thompson stepped down into the roadway's dust. "Another thought to take to bed with you, too; I'm keeping that shovel handy. Good night."

"Good night."

Ben watched the marshal amble across the road, heading for his combination office-jail-and-residence. He made a cigarette, smoked it in the gloom of the hotel's narrow doorway, then he pinched it out and went up to his room.

He kicked out of his boots, hung his shell-belt on the bedpost close to hand, and threw himself down upon the coverlet. The night seemed old and tired; not like it had seemed on the ridge with Sarahlee; old and tired like his body. There was a tightness in him he could not share with it. The tightness that went with killing; it wasn't related in any way to fear; it was the tightness of a coiled spring; the tightness of challenge and of approaching death, for someone.

CHAPTER FOUR

Shortly after dawn of the next day, Ben got his horse from the liverybarn and rode north-west. When he was near the foothills, he began quartering for fresh-horse-sign. There was none, so he rode still farther back, keeping a flinty ridge between him and the Marlow place. Not until he crept stealthily down to the forbidden road afoot, did he find what he sought. The imprints of a newly-shod horse. He traced out the imprint of the blacksmith's stamp, with his finger in the dust, then he went back to his horse, made a cigarette and smoked it, watching the road. No one passed by in either direction, but he was satisfied, and finally, he returned to Deming.

It was early afternoon, the town was full of ranch-wagons, riders, and townsfolk. After putting up his horse, he took a seat in the shade outside the barn, tilted his hat forward to shield his eyes, and sat like stone, watching people pass. He was still sitting like that an hour later when Cliff Thompson came across him.

"You out of your mind, sitting here like a plain target?"

Ben sat up, pushed his hat back, and spat. "No, I don't think so. Mr. Bushwhacker won't be coming to town today."

Thompson teetered forward, staring. "You found him; you two had it out already?"

"No, I haven't met him yet, but I know where he is — and to me, that's more important."

"How come?" the marshal asked, sinking down on the bench beside Ben.

"It confirms what I've been thinking."

"Like what?"

"Never mind, Marshal. If I told you, we'd both know, and that'd spoil things for me."

Thompson swore. "I had two posses looking for him. Where is he?"

Ben got up, squinted at the sun, and started away. Thompson went after him. When they both got on the far plankwalk, Ben said, "I'll let you know in a couple of days."

"That's obstructing justice, Ben."

"Nope; that's life insurance — mine," Ben said, and went up to his room.

He went down to the diner for supper a

little after seven o'clock. It was still daylight. For the first time he noticed people looking at him, speaking softly to one another as he ate. Later, outside again, eyes followed him to the liverybarn. When he rode out, northerly, he could feel the faces watching him. When he stopped where the stage-road made a bend — where he'd seen the runabout parked the night before — and sat there hidden by the scraggly oaks, he thought of Joel Partin and wagged his head. It only took one loose tongue to set a town buzzing.

The wait wasn't long. As soon as he could make out the yellow wheels and the blazed-face horse, he urged his mount forward, partially blocking the road. When the rig stopped he touched his hat and said, "Evening, ma'm. Need more thread?"

Instead of replying, Sarahlee swung the buggy towards the oaks. Ben followed. When she stopped, he got down, tied both horses, went back and leaned on the dashboard looking up.

"Mighty nice night."

"Mr. Roan, he's back. He's up at the ranch."

"Is that so," Ben said mildly, admiring the way her eyes flashed, the way her blouse rose and fell. "When's he coming to town, ma'm?"

"I don't know. It'll be within the next day or two."

"What's the delay?"

"He told Uncle Will he wants his horse to rest up a day or two."

"Does he know the marshal's looking for him?"

Sarahlee's eyes widened hopefully. "Is he? I mean . . ."

"Had two posses out yesterday, ma'm. Sent telegrams to the towns around." Ben held out his hand. Sarahlee put hers into it and got down. Ben didn't release the hand and she turned towards him, making no attempt to pull it away. "I knew he was up there, ma'm. 'Rode up a ways this morning and found his sign." He let go of her hand. "It clinched this thing for me."

"You mean about my uncle and my cousins?" He nodded. "There's something else, too . . . But I'm not going to tell you. I can't — it wouldn't be right. I've already done enough."

He nodded at her gently, "I know you have. You've done more than I had any right to ask you to do. More than most women would have done." He took her arm and guided her back towards the moon drenched ridge. "I can guess the rest, anyway."

She pulled free and faced him. "What? What can you guess?"

"That your cousins'll be with him when he comes for me in Deming."

She nodded woodenly, averting her face. "That's it. That's it, Mr. Roan." Her eyes sought his. "I've helped you, haven't I?"

"Yes'm. You've probably saved my life."

"Then, can I ask a favour of you?"

"Yes'm. Only, I can't do it."

"Do what?"

"I think you're going to ask me to do one of two things; either saddle up and ride away, or avoid a fight with your cousins."

"You could. You could saddle up before dawn tomorrow and be far away by the time they got to town." Her fingers closed over his arm. "It would save lives. Not just theirs, but yours too."

The night-silence thickened between them. Ben reached up, took her hand off his arm, and held her by the shoulders. "I don't want to fight Hal or El. I don't even feel mad towards old Will. But they're calling this dance, Sarahlee, I'm not, and running'd cost me more'n self-respect, it'd cost me my ranch. I'm sorry, but I'll stick around for a while yet."

"But — supposing Rockwell comes to

Deming tomorrow?"

"Why, I suppose one of us'll stay there permanently."

"But the boys'll be with him. Think of the odds."

"I've thought of 'em, ma'm."

"You won't have a chance."

"I think the odds are pretty nearly even. You see, I know they're coming, and they figure they're going to catch me unawares. That sort of evens things up."

She opened her mouth to protest and Ben bent on a sudden impulse and kissed her. She braced against the pressure of his mouth and when he moved back, she stared at him, dumbfounded, for a moment, then she put the back of one hand across her mouth and a stormy look came over her face, but it didn't stay. When she let the hand fall away she said, "Well . . . !"

"I wanted to do that last night."

"Well . . . Why didn't you?"

"I was afraid to. You were on the prod last night."

"You don't think I am tonight?"

"No'm, I don't think so." To cover confusion, he reached for his tobacco sack, began worrying up a cigarette.

"Was that out of gratitude, Ben?"

"Gratitude? Ma'm, I never kissed anybody

out of gratitude in my life."

"But you've kissed them . . ."

"Not like you, I haven't," he said, holding the cigarette, making no move to light it. "I don't ever expect to again, either." He looked down at the cigarette, blinked at it, and let it fall from his hand. "I guess I'll tell you what I was thinking last night." He waited, she kept looking at him. "Well, when that horse threw you . . ."

"You straightened my clothes."

He flushed. "I wasn't thinking of that. I was thinking of how the sun shone off your hair, and how your face looked in the shade of my hat. And later, when we were eating, how you looked when you got mad. And again, when you knelt at the creek and washed the pans. And even last night, ma'm, when you kept turning your back on me. Last night, particularly; you're just about the prettiest woman I ever saw, Sarahlee. . . . Last night I was thinking you were the loveliest woman I ever saw. But I never used that word before, and I wasn't plumb sure how you'd take it . . ."

"I like it, Ben. I like it very much. Do you know something else? I liked that kiss. And as long as we're confessing . . . Do you remember when you grabbed my arm when Hal was in the road? Well, I wasn't afraid someone was going to be killed . . . I was afraid it would be *you* . . . I was afraid your hold on my arm wouldn't be there."

The night around them was silent and warm. A melancholy moon rode high overhead, and far off a coyote called, a sound full of age-old sadness. He put the tobacco sack back in his pocket in a business-like fashion, reached out and drew her against him, and for a moment it was hard to breathe, then he bent his head, hers came up, and they kissed again. Finally, she pushed against his chest and said, "I've got to get back."

He went to the buggy with her, helped her up and when she was seated she bent forward, cupped his face between her palms and said, "Ben, I didn't want you to ride away, not really. I just didn't want you killed." She drew back and took up the lines. "Tomorrow will be the seventeenth. . . ."

"And tomorrow night I'll meet you up by the seepage spring."

She looked down quickly, startled. "Not there. That's too close to the house."

"Sarahlee, another night or two like this and your cousins're going to be trailing after you. Even a man can figure out that no one needs *that* much thread." His grin warmed her. "About this time or earlier, at the seepage spring."

"Yes," she said, and drove down towards the road.

He mounted, waited until the buggy was gone, then rode slowly back to Deming. He was in his room, boots off and shell-belt hanging from the bedpost, when a short rap of knuckles brought him up facing the door.

"Who is it?"

"Bell — the lawyer."

He opened the door with his gun held low, let Bell in, un-cocked the weapon and tossed it on the bed. "Up kind of late, aren't you, Mr. Bell."

"It's urgent."

"Well, sit down," Ben said, dropping back down on the edge of the bed. "What's bothering you?"

"Marshal Thompson came by my office this evening. He was making up a posse."

"That's his right, isn't it?"

"Yes, but he said you told him about this gunman the Marlows hired to kill you."

"I didn't tell Marshal Thompson any such a damned thing, and he knows it."

Bell gestured with one hand. "I didn't mean you told him in so many words; I meant something you said told him where this gunman is."

Ben straightened up. "Where? You mean he took a posse and ——"

"He went up to the Marlow place. He said things you'd said convinced him that was the only place the killer could be; that his two posses had failed to find this man, and you rode right to where he was, and that meant he had to be up at the Marlow place. I drew up a peace bond and had him take it along, to give ——"

"Wait a minute. Thompson's gone up to Marlow's to arrest Rockwell?"

Bell nodded. "He also said he might bring them all back, for harbouring a criminal. Of course he'd have trouble making that stick. All they have to do is say they didn't know Rockwell was a criminal."

"What a damn-fool move," Ben said. "How long can he hold any of 'em — even Rockwell? A week, ten days, no more'n that, and I'll lay you odds Marlow's lawyer gets 'em all out on bond before breakfast time tomorrow." He got up, walked to the wash-stand and back again. "How long ago did he leave?"

Before Bell could reply the clatter of horsemen riding into town echoed in the stillness. Ben cocked his head a moment, looked at Bell, then strode to the window and leaned out. Deming was still; even the saloons were quiet. People lined the sidewalks. There was a little movement among them, but hardly any talk.

The horsemen, with Marshal Thompson in the lead, walked their horses through the dust of the roadway. Beside Thompson, tied across the saddle of a led-horse, was the body of a man. Ben strained to see but the night-shadows of the roadway made it difficult. He stepped back, shot Bell a look, and spoke as he reached for his shell-belt. "They're back and it looks like they got their man."

He dumped the six-gun into its holster, sat down long enough to tug on his boots, then started for the door. Bell was close behind. They went down the stairs side by side. When they came out onto the plank-walk the posse was dismounting down by the marshal's office, and the watchers were drifting that way, the sound of their talk rising over the clank of armed men dismounting at the marshal's hitchrack, mumbling among themselves, grunting under the limp burden of a broken body.

Ben left Bell and edged through the mob. A tall man with a carbine stopped him near the office door. "No visitors," he said. "If you want to see the marshal come around tomorrow."

A wizened Texan standing in the shadows close by spat amber liquid into the dust and said, "Never figured Thompson to be the 'doing' kind, always thought him to be the 'talkin' ' kind." A thick-set shadow behind him grunted something unintelligible as Ben was turning away; only his last words were clear: ". . . looked like the youngest 'un to me." Ben halted, came slowly around and stared at the speaker. He was in the act of going towards the man when his name was called. He looked back. Marshal Thompson was standing there, his face in the shadows, his legs wide-spread. "Come on in, Ben."

The crowd made way and Ben followed Thompson into the office, which was crowded with men. A powerful smell of horse-sweat, tobacco, and coffee, filled the room. The rough conversation dwindled as Ben pushed his way through, and stood by the cot where the dead man lay. The boyish face of Guy Marlow looked up at him, peacefully relaxed and with no sign of injury. Ben looked across the cot where Cliff Thompson was standing.

"What happened?"

"We rode up and called out. The kid opened up on us." Thompson's eyes were level and unmoving. "I think he thought it was someone else. I think he thought it was just one man — someone in particular he figured would ride up there for a fight. We fired back — waited a while, and when no more shots came from the house, we rushed it." Thompson's hand gestured slightly. "There he was, behind a window. A bullet had peeled off a long splinter from the sill and drove into his head behind the ear. He was dead."

"Where were the others?"

Thompson shrugged. "We never saw 'em, but we waited around for 'em. Finally, we came back."

"Nice night's work," Ben said, gazing at the corpse. "I guess you know what'll happen now."

"He didn't give us much choice, Ben."

"I reckon he didn't," Ben said, turning away.

"Ben . . ."

"Yeah?"

"We met Sarahlee when we were coming back."

Ben moved over closer to the cot again, his eyes on the marshal's face. "And?"

"She saw the kid . . . She said a lot of things . . ."

"Like?"

"Like you knew we were going up there,

88

and kept her down here deliberately . . .
Like the kid didn't know what was going on
and we killed him without giving him a
chance . . . Things like that."

Ben looked at Guy Marlow's face for a
long time, then he returned his gaze to the
marshal and said, "Well, Cliff, like I said,
you did a nice night's work."

He went back outside, walked across the
road to the bench outside the Oases and sat
down in the darkness, watching the slow-
strolling throng moving away from the
marshal's office, some towards home, others towards the saloons.

Charley Bell came up, squinted down at
him, then sat down. "Was it really the kid?"

"Yes."

Bell blew out a long sigh. "And after all
the talk the marshal's been putting out
about not wanting trouble."

"Yeah."

"Well, I guess that's the way the cards fall,
sometimes."

"Yeah."

Bell looked around, studied the craggy
profile a moment, then arose, said "Good
night," got no reply, and moved off into the
darkness.

He was still sitting there an hour later
when the last of the posse left the marshal's

office, and Thompson, in the company of two riders, crossed the road to the Oases. When the marshal saw Ben sitting there, legs thrust out and eyes fixed on nothing, he motioned the others on into the saloon and sank down on the edge of the bench.

"It couldn't be helped, Ben."

"Maybe not. Did you sing out that you wanted Rockwell?"

"He didn't give us a chance. As soon as I 'hallooed' the house he cut loose. The boys fired back. It was all over in ten seconds."

"You bought yourself a man-sized war, Thompson; I expect you know that."

"Like I said, I didn't have any other choice."

"I reckon you didn't; take fifteen men up there to kill one kid. I reckon you had your duty to do."

The marshal's face hardened and his eyes grew still. "I been trying to explain to you; he didn't give us a chance to tell him what we wanted."

Ben got up, nodded, and walked down towards the hotel doorway. Marshal Thompson looked after him, unmoving, until several sage-scented riders came up and got him to join them in a drink, then he disappeared beyond the Oases' spindle-hinged doors.

Ben tried to sleep but the picture of Guy Marlow's face was spiked to the back wall of his eyelids. He tossed until Deming grew quiet, then he sat up and smoked. Beyond the town scavenging coyotes howled. He listened for a while then, shortly before sunup, he washed, shaved, got dressed and left the hotel. Outside, the new day was still, fragrant, and benignly cool. He went to the liverybarn, got his horse and rode northward out of town at a walk. Two hours later, with the sun warming and the coral newness turning yellow, he dismounted among some willows and knelt to drink at the farthest extremity of Roan Creek, where it lost itself on the prairie a mile from the foothills. He was arising, turning towards his horse, when a shout quivered in the dead air. He spun around, searching the distance. The shout was repeated, and that time he saw them. Three riders coming towards him from the direction of Deming in a belly-down run.

He recognised Thompson first, and the last man, even without the cinnamon derby, would have been Charley Bell; he rode with his elbows flopping like wings. The man in between was tall, whipcord-thin, and rode like a centaur. Ben did not recognise him until he was close enough to begin slowing; it was Deming Town Marshal Jake Gibbel, who frequently rode with Thompson and had, in fact, been one of the posse leaders the night before.

The marshal reined up first, his horse setting-up under a light hand on a good spade bit. Gibbel was next, and the last to rein up was Charley Bell, who looked relieved the race was ended.

Thompson said, "Where are you going?"

Ben jerked his head sideways to indicate the foothills. "Up there. Why?"

"To the Marlows?"

Ben shrugged and said nothing.

Thompson dismounted. "Listen; in the first place they'll kill you. In the second place, you can't ride up that road — you know that — not until the court's decided whether you got the right or not."

Ben looked from Thompson to Gibbel. The Town Marshal was woodenly impassive. Beyond him, Charley Bell was fidgeting in the saddle. "I don't have to use that road," Ben said, finally. "There are a dozen different ways to get back into the hills from here."

Thompson was looking northward, and he was scowling. "I ought to arrest you," he said. "At least that'd keep trouble from starting in a new direction."

Ben grunted and squatted in the shade.

"You're not thinking very straight, Marshal. You've already started all the trouble you can handle. Maybe even more'n you can handle."

"Well, you riding up there won't help matters any."

"It might. I had an offer in mind, to make the Marlows."

"What kind of an offer?"

"It doesn't matter now. Look, Marshal, up to now the Marlows have been playing a waiting game. They haven't even shown themselves in town. They've been avoiding me like poison. They've been waiting to see what the court decides. Up until last night you had a better than even chance to keep the peace; now you have no chance at all. Even coyotes'll fight when you kill their young."

"You sure make it sound like it's all my fault."

"It is, Marshal. The Marlows were waiting, and I was going along. I didn't like it — but I was doing it. Even their hired gunman might not have caused trouble. I got a notion he wouldn't have."

"Why wouldn't he have; just tell me that?"

"Sure, because I meant to stay out of his way, that's why. I didn't want trouble any more than you did. I wanted to live here —

not make a battleground out of the country-side. That's the only reason why I went along with your peace-policy. Even if I'd met Rockwell, it'd have been a short fight. But after what you did last night, believe me, Marshal, that's all changed."

"Dammit, I *told* you the kid gave us no choice."

"I'm not saying he did; what I'm saying is, there's going to be a war, and nothing you or I can do is going to stop it." Ben looked up towards the purple-forested hills. "There wouldn't have been any bloodshed, Marshal. Not even after I'd finished my cabin up there. Oh, there'd have been plenty of tall-talk, and maybe a bushwhacking shot or two, but that's about all it'd have amounted to. I tried to tell you that when I first came to town."

"So now you were going to ride up there peaceable-like, and get yourself killed, and really clinch things."

"I don't think they'd kill me. I wanted to tell Will he can have the Roan place." Ben tapped his shirt. "I've got the patent right here."

"He wouldn't take it, now."

"Maybe not. I just wanted to make a try."

The marshal pulled his reins through his fingers and snapped them. He was frowning. "I don't think even the law could ride up there today, without a battle; otherwise I'd offer to take the patent up for you."

"Thanks," Ben said dryly, getting to his feet. "I don't need the law to mind my business for me."

Thompson continued to frown in thought. "I guess there's more to it, from your viewpoint, than you've told us here."

"There is."

"Well, I tried to tell her what happened. She was so worked up I didn't get the chance." Thompson raised his glance. "That's what you meant, wasn't it?"

"Yes."

Town Marshal Gibbel cleared his throat. "If you fellers're talking about Miz' Sarahlce — her paw's coming up from Santa Fe in a couple days. Him and me used to ride together, years back. He wrote me 'bout a week back sayin' he was comin' up to fetch her back home."

"All that means," Marshal Thompson said glumly, "is that there'll be another Marlow on the prod. Damn! I'd give a lot to be able to re-live last night." He turned, sprang into the saddle and motioned to Ben. "You're coming back with us. I hope you're going to be sensible about it . . ."

Ben went to his horse and mounted. He

sat there gazing at the three men a moment, then he reined around and started towards Deming.

Thompson and Gibbel rode ahead a little distance and Charley Bell rode beside Ben. From time to time he cast a glance at the man beside him. Finally he said, "If you meant what you said about wanting to avoid a fight with Rockwell, you could get Cliff to lock you up for a few days."

"You know better than that, Bell."

They continued on for a while in silence, then Bell tried again. "Suppose, as your attorney, I went to the Marlows . . ."

"You've got a one-track mind," Ben said. "There's only one way to settle the personal end of this, and that's man to man. You take care of the court-end of things and leave the rest to me."

"But you said you wanted to avoid —"

"It's too late now, Bell."

"This girl Cliff was talking about — is she the one from Santa Fe who's staying — ?"

"You heard what Gibbel said, didn't you?" Ben said shortly.

"Uh, yes. Cliff implied you were friendly with her."

"I am — I was. Listen, Bell —"

"All right; all right, Mr. Roan. I was just

trying to make conversation, is all."

"You don't have to make it for me."

They rode the rest of the way back to Deming in silence. At the liverybarn, where Gibbel and Bell left them, the marshal and Ben Roan stood in the sunblast watching their animals being led away. Thompson turned, shook himself like a dog coming out a creek, and blew his breath out noisily. "More trouble," he said, and pointed towards the Oases as Ben turned. "That yellow-wheeled rig at the rack there; that's Will Marlow's outfit."

As Thompson started forward Ben's fingers grazed his arm. "I'll make you a bet, Marshal. I'll give you odds old Will didn't drive that rig down here."

Thompson looked from the buggy to Ben and nodded. "You're on," he said. "The only reason I'm betting is because I want you to be right."

Ben watched Thompson go past the Marlow rig, eye it a moment, then push into the Oases, then he also crossed the road, but heading for the stairway to his room.

CHAPTER FIVE

Ben took a firm grip on the door-latch of his room, lifted it and thrust the door swiftly inward. No shot came out to greet him; instead, Sarahlee turned away from the window to meet his glance. Her face was pale, and the expression on it was both pale and resolute. Ben closed the door, took off his hat and flung it on the dresser.

"I wasn't expecting you, exactly," he said. "When I saw the buggy I thought it'd be Rockwell waiting for me."

"If it had been, you'd be dead by now. I watched you and the marshal ride up to the liverybarn. If I'd been Jake Rockwell I'd have shot you through this window."

"I reckon you would have at that." He studied her face a moment, then crossed to the bed and sat down. "I think you know I had nothing to do with what happened, Sarahlee."

She remained standing, for a moment her

glance went back to the window, and beyond, out over the shimmering town. "I don't think you did," she said quietly. "At first I wasn't sure, but now I don't believe you knew it was going to happen." She leaned back upon the wall, a little to one side of the window. "Did you see him when they brought him back?"

"Yes."

"Was he badly mutilated?"

"No; in fact a splinter of wood killed him, not a bullet. It went into his head behind the left ear. He looked as natural as always. Like he was asleep."

"You know what will happen now, don't you?"

"I can guess."

"They started this morning. They all rode up to Roan's Creek and burned you out."

"Where were they last night when the posse rode up there?"

"Setting up relays for Rockwell to use after he's killed you."

"And when's he going to do that?"

She shook her head at him. "I don't know, but I don't think, after what's happened, Uncle Will can put it off any longer than today — if he wanted to — and he doesn't want to. He went wild last night; it took both Hal and El to keep him from riding down here after you himself."

"I reckon," Ben said. "Why haven't they come for Guy's body?"

"That's why I came. The doctor is embalming it for me right now."

"And you're going to take it back up there to be buried?"

She shook her head a second time, looking down at him in an impersonal way. "No, he's going to be buried next to his mother, here in town."

"Well," he said, arising, "I expect the best thing for me to do is ride out a ways and meet them."

She moved off the wall, stood straight and stiff. "Four of them? Are you out of your mind?"

"Maybe that's it. I just don't feel very good about things, Sarahlee. Guy wasn't in it; besides, he was only a kid." He looked around at her. "You know, I started up there this morning to give your uncle my patent to the Roan place . . ."

"You wouldn't have found them there. But if you had they wouldn't have listened — not to you — not now, Ben."

"That's what Thompson said. So, I guess I owe old Will a chance at me, at least."

"Ben, it wasn't your fault. You mustn't feel this way." She crossed to his side, stood there trying to see into his face.

"It isn't only Guy," he said. "It's all the rest of it. This law-court business over the road, the burning-out, the killing, the hired gunman . . . It's the whole stinking mess, Sarahlee, and before it's over, unless I ride out and end it myself, it might spread to the townsmen. It's happened before; folks taking sides in feuds; getting killed over nothing." He crossed to the dresser, took up his hat and asked: "Which way did they go, after they left Roan's Creek?"

"Easterly. Please listen to me, Ben . . ."

He scowled. "Easterly? There's no road over there, Sarahlee."

"I didn't say there was."

"You said they were fixing relays for Rockwell. To the east there's nothing but mountains and a trailless waste."

"I don't know why, but that's the way they went. Perhaps Rockwell wanted it that way; after all, he's a professional killer; he'd know the best way to get away, wouldn't he?"

"He might think that's the best way, because he'd be hard to find up there. What he doesn't know is that he could kill ten horses trying to find his way out of those mountains."

"I don't care what becomes of him, and you shouldn't either." She took his hand, held it in both of hers. "At least take the marshal with you, Ben."

"He wouldn't go, knowing I meant to fight. He's against this kind of fighting."

She dropped his hand, and her eyes flashed. "Is he! He started it, didn't he?"

"I reckon. Sarahlee, would you do me a favour? I'd like to talk to you when I get back. I want you to hear my side of what happens, first. Not like last night." He put the hat on. "I want you to stick around town until I'm back. Will you do that?"

"I'll wait, Ben."

"And Sarahlee . . ."

"I understand, Ben. I'd give my right arm if it didn't have to be this way, but I understand."

He left her in his room. Back outside, on the plankwalk, he was aware of how passers-by looked at him; how riders in the roadway spoke aside to their companions as they went past. Charley Bell came hurrying up waving a slip of paper.

"The judge'll be here tomorrow, Ben."

"Good for him," Ben said, gazing intently towards the liverybarn. "Seen the marshal around?"

"No. He's probably over at his office." Bell's hand dropped to his side. "Where are you going?"

"For a ride," Ben said, stepping down off the walk and heading for the barn. The lawyer watched him for a short moment, then scurried towards the marshal's office.

Ben was swinging into the saddle when Cliff Thompson's voice sounded from the barn's entrance. "Listen, Ben, dammit all, I don't want to lock you up, but I will if you force me to."

"I haven't broken any laws, Marshal," Ben said, shortening the reins.

"But you're sure going to. I can tell by the look on your face."

Ben urged the horse as far as the doorway, and stopped. "That must be a new law," he said. "I didn't know you could arrest a man for the way he looked." When Thompson started to speak, Ben cut him off. "And I see Joel Partin's not your only watchdog around Deming."

"Never mind that. Where are you going?"

"For a ride; any objections?"

"I can guess where."

"You're a pretty good guesser then, because I'm not sure myself. But I'll tell you one thing, I'm not going up to Marlow's or Roan's Creek."

Thompson squinted up at Ben. Uncertainty was stamped across his face. Finally he said, "Well . . . Listen, Ben, do us both a favour . . ."

Ben smiled without mirth, touched his hat-brim, and urged his horse out into the scorching-hot roadway. Marshal Thompson stood in the barn's opening, frowning after him. When he finally turned away, a soft voice hailed him and for a moment he couldn't locate it. Then he saw Sarahlee leaning out the window of Ben's room at the hotel, and walked closer, staring upwards.

"Follow him, Marshal. He's going to meet my uncle and his hired killer."

Thompson didn't wait; he spun around, trotted into the liverybarn, and while he was saddling, he told the hostler to run and fetch Charley Bell. By the time Ben's lawyer got to the barn the marshal was mounted and waiting.

"Get up a posse, Charley, and send them after me. I'll try to keep Roan in sight, and I'll go slow enough for the posse-boys to find me. Hurry."

Bell scuttled away and Cliff Thompson bucketed out of Deming in a slow-lope. At first he did not see Ben, and if he hadn't topped a rise when he did, he never would have seen him, because Ben was loping into a nearby fingerling of trees. The marshal made a hard smile, jerked his mount towards the nearest scrub-oak thicket, rode in and stopped. He sat there a full ten minutes, then he edged out and loped straight towards the trees where Ben Roan had disappeared.

When Ben was satisfied no one was trailing him, he turned easterly and kept within the fringe of forest as long as he could, following around the base of the mountains. He'd been riding two hours before he topped out on a hill above Roan's Creek. There, looking down upon the black ruin of his cabin, he smoked a cigarette. Later, another two miles farther on, he cut fresh horse-sign, and although he got down frequently to study it, the imprints were too faint for him to make out whether Joel Partin's stamp was on one of the sets of shoes, or not.

After that, he paralleled the tracks northerly, and tried to use every vantage point to see ahead. But the farther east he rode, the thicker grew the trees, and only once did he get a clear view, and that time there was nothing moving as far as he could see.

He rode steadily until the sun was directly overhead and the scent of pine-sap was heavy, then a horse nickered somewhere ahead and he instantly flung himself from the saddle and caught his own mount by the nostrils to prevent it answering. When the danger was past, he rode back a half mile, tied his horse among some trees, and retraced his steps afoot.

Scouting with caution, Ben found the horse, rump to him, tied among some second-growth fir trees. He scouted the locale, satisfied himself the horse was alone, then went forward to examine it. The clear imprint of a W M brand on the beast's left shoulder established the fact of ownership to Ben's satisfaction. He untied the horse, slapped it on the ribs and watched it dodge and twist through the trees heading for home.

When he was riding again, feeling pleased that he had released one of Rockwell's escape animals, he continued on easterly. The land became more rocky, more tangled with underbrush, harder to penetrate. He dropped down lower, hoping to find easier going, and while crossing a sage-girt clearing, he sighted a rider disappearing into the trees a quarter mile ahead. Reining back into the covert, Ben unshipped his carbine, rested it across his lap, scrutinised the land ahead for other riders, saw none, and began a slow advance.

Where the land dropped almost to the rangeland beyond, there was a fifty-acre mesa called Horse Flat. He remembered hunting there with his father years before. He also recalled that, from Horse Flat, a person had an excellent view of the country north of Deming. Leaving his horse again, he scouted the mesa afoot, and near its easterly extremity, where the sage and buckbrush fringed it, he saw two men talking, standing beside their horses. One of them gestured westerly with a sweep of his arm. The other man looked around, then said something and turned to mount. The first man, whom Ben recognised as he crept closer, as El Marlow, said something else and the stranger paused, looked over his shoulder, caught sight of Ben and snapped a clear, sharp warning. El Marlow dove for the brush and the stranger yanked his horse around so that it was between his body and Ben. The glint of steel shone under the animal's neck as Ben called out:

"Drop it!"

The stranger fired instead. Ben ducked away from the blast. As he was creeping through the brush two more shots shattered the stillness. He tried to place the first one, which had come from El Marlow's gun. The stranger was gone; his horse looked around, bewildered, and snorted softly.

"Roan! Hey, Roan!"

Ben was rolling as he answered, knowing they'd fire at the sound of his voice. "Yeah." He wasn't wrong; two slamming shots rolled out, their echoes rising into the heat of the mesa.

"Stand up and fight, Roan."

He made no reply; kept edging towards the east end of the mesa, stopping now and then, seeking movement. There was none.

"The Old Man's behind you, Roan. Him and Hal . . . They'll get you sure, if we don't . . . How do you like the odds, Roan? About like you gave Guy, aren't they?"

Ben got behind a granite boulder, fired three rapid shots at the sound of Marlow's voice, then, as he was reloading, he called out, "I had nothing to do with what happened to Guy. I wasn't with the posse, and I didn't hear about it until they brought him back to Deming."

"You're a damned liar!"

"As for Hal and the Old Man," Ben went on, unruffled, "Do you think I just happened to be up here, El? I expected to find all of you together . . . And yeah, I like the odds; I even like the idea of Rockwell being there with you. Four-to-one's about right. Four bushwhackers, El . . . Takes a lot of guts to burn a man's cabin when he's not around. Takes a lot of guts to stake horses out for a drygulcher."

"Hey, Roan," a deep-booming and unfamiliar voice called out. "How'd you know my name?"

"Easy, Rockwell. The same way everybody else around Deming knows it — off the wanted posters you had in your saddlebags."

There was a long, tense silence. Ben strained to hear; he knew Rockwell and El Marlow would be deep in conversation. But he was too far away. Leaving the boulder, Ben began to crawl forward on all-fours. When he came to a narrow erosion gully, he lay in it full length, waiting. When nothing happened he pushed his carbine forward and let off a shot. Instantly two shots came back, both high and to his right. He lowered his own sights, fired, levered, and fired again. That time a veritable fusillade came back. Ben kept his head down and pressed hard against the ground. Bullets cut the brush around him, then the racket died away and the deep-booming voice called out

"Roan? I'll walk out in the clearing — you walk out — and the best man walks away. How about it?"

"Sure; just as soon as El stands up and shucks his guns."

Silence again. Ben smiled to himself. After

a time he said, "What's the matter, Rockwell; your pardner lose his guts?"

A shot slashed the brush above Ben's gully. He laughed out loud. "El, you couldn't hit the side of a barn if you were inside it. Come on, Rockwell; I'm waiting."

El Marlow answered with a snarl. "So are we, and we're better fixed for waiting than you are, Roan. The Old Man and Hal'll hear the shooting. They'll get you from behind."

"I kind of hope they do, El. I'd like to get this over with when you're all together." When El did not speak again, Ben became suspicious. "Rockwell? How about that stand-up fight?" The stillness persisted. " 'Want to earn your blood-money, don't you?" Still no answer. Ben rolled out of the gully and began crawling northward, away from the mesa. There was a knoll, brushed-over except for its wind-swept top, jutting up out of the undergrowth several hundred yards to his left. He made for it, hoping to be able to see down from its eminence. Sweat darkened his shirt and stung his eyes as he crawled towards it, careful to avoid disturbing the brush.

Twenty nerve-racking minutes went by, then El called out again. "Roan? Hey, Roan? Rockwell's ready to fight you." The silence dragged on and Marlow, sensing something,

110

raised his voice to a shrill cry. "Roan! What's the matter — you scared?"

Ben kept crawling, hearing but not heeding the calls and curses of El Marlow. Then, when stillness returned, he halted, lay flat and rested. The knoll was less than five hundred yards ahead. When he was raising up to go forward again, the deep voice of Jake Rockwell called to him.

"Roan, we'll do like you want. El'll shuck his gun and I'll walk out into the clearing."

Ben twisted around. Rockwell's voice had come from the direction of the gully where he had been lying.

"Well, dammit, Roan; are you going to ante up, or not?"

Ben made no reply. Clearly, they were trying to draw him out; to keep him talking while they got him between them. He searched for a stone, found one and tossed it overhand far to the right. Instantly Rockwell fired where the brush quivered. Ben threw three more stones into the same brush-clump and Rockwell fired twice more. When the last echo faded, Ben tossed two more stones, larger this time, and the brush-clump rattled and quivered as they went through it.

"I got him! By God, El, I got him! He's west of you there, where the brush shook.

He's lyin' over there kicking."

When El answered Rockwell, Ben was startled; his voice came back from the east side of the knoll. Apparently El had also been crawling towards the little hill. "Wait, Jake; wait'll I can look down in there."

"You know which brush-clump?"

"Yeah, I saw it shake."

Ben rolled over, thrust his carbine forward and waited. He saw no movement up the side of the knoll until El was near the top, then sunlight quivered along his carbine barrel. Ben drew his own gun snug against his shoulder, shook sweat out of his eyes, and inched the barrel up.

First, El held his gun out, then his arm, then he darted a quick look out of the brush and withdrew his head. Rockwell's curses floated through the hush.

"What you scared of, dammit; I seen him kicking over there like a gut-shot deer."

El emerged into the clearing atop the knoll, crouched over and with both hands holding his carbine. Ben drew in a big breath, let it out slowly, and squeezed the trigger. The muzzle-blast bracketed out-wards seconds ahead of El Marlow's high, piercing scream. He fell in a heap and shale-dust rose around him.

Rockwell's voice rose in a string of oaths.

He emptied his six-gun in the direction of Ben's solitary shot. Two of the slugs whined close and when stillness returned, a twig fell on Ben's gun-barrel; he flicked it off, rolled over and began crawling back the way he had come, towards the gully. It was painfully slow work. When he got there, the gully was empty. A number of sparkling brass casings lay in the depression. While he was examining them, and following Rockwell's trail through the brush with his eyes, he heard a horse grunt. This was followed by the slap of leather, then the dull thunder of a saddle-animal running. He started to get up. A shot kept him from raising his head, then he heard Rockwell's mount hit the brush with a tearing sound.

By the time he dared look out over the sage, Rockwell was gone; even the echo of his passing was lost. Ben squatted, re-loaded his guns, and started towards the knoll, this time walking upright, but in a crouch, twisting and bending through the undergrowth. Before he got to the top he heard movement above and stopped. The sound of shattered breathing came clearly to him. He got down low, circled to the right, and came into view of the eminence behind the downed man.

Marlow was trying to sit up. He had a

cocked six-gun in one fist — his left one. Moving forward on the balls of his feet, Ben was less than twenty feet away when he said, "Drop it, El!"

Marlow tried to turn. A sob came out of him. Ben went up close, bent down and wrenched the gun away, uncocked it and knelt down beside the injured man. "Bleeding pretty bad, isn't it?"

"You dirty son —"

"Whoa! This was your idea, not mine. Hold it out."

"I can't. It's broke."

Ben holstered his pistol, laid his carbine aside and made a sling for Marlow's broken right arm with their two belts. Then he fashioned a bandage from handkerchiefs and slowed the gush of blood. When he was finished, he dragged Marlow into the shade and propped him against a rock, squatted down and thumbed back his hat.

"Your friend's gone."

Marlow glared malevolently. His jaws were locked tight against the pain that was making him half-sick.

"I could've killed you just as easy, El."

"Why didn't you?"

Ben rocked back on his heels. "No need," he said.

"You'll live to wish you had, Roan. Believe

me, you will."

"Maybe. Your horse ran off. I'm going after mine. He's tied back a ways. You sit still until I get back, then we'll head for Deming."

"You'll never get there. Paw and Hal'll are close by."

"Yeah?" Ben said, getting up. "Why didn't they help you, then?"

"They're probably waiting for a clean shot at you."

Ben wagged his head. "I doubt it, El. I'm as good a target right now as they could want — no one's shooting." Marlow's slitted eyes showed arrow-points of hatred. Ben spoke again. "No point in us kidding each other, El. Will and Hal aren't around."

"You think not, huh?"

"Yeah. They're staking out the other horses for Rockwell's get-away. Now just take it easy until I get back. Don't go moving around or you'll start that thing bleeding again. You'll be sick enough by the time we get to town; don't take a chance on bleeding-out." Ben stooped, picked up Marlow's guns, and moved off, westerly.

By the time he got back to his horse thirst and weariness were bothering him. He drank from the canteen on the saddle, made a cigarette, smoked it while he rested, then he snugged up the cinch, mounted, and started back towards the knoll. He was near the mesa when he heard voices. Stopping in the shade of a ragged juniper, he got down cautiously, and crept forward until he had a good view of the knoll and the mesa beyond. Within his view, but hidden from El Marlow, a man was holding four horses. Nearer, pushing their way through the brush up the slope, three men were cursing and climbing. El Marlow's voice encouraged them with alternating oaths and entreaties.

"Hurry up, Paw. Dammit, he got me — busted my arm near the shoulder. I'm bleedin' like a stuck hog. Hal? Rockwell lit out. Come on, I got to have some water . . ."

Ben was close enough to see the first man who topped out on the knoll. He recognised him instantly, and so did El Marlow, whose mouth dropped open in surprise.

"Marshal . . ."

"Yeah. Hello, El. So he got you, did he? Well, that's one less for me to worry about."

"Where's my paw? Where's —"

"I don't know," Cliff Thompson said, casting a hard look out over the brush. "And I don't care. The man I'm after is Ben Roan. How long ago did he leave?"

"Just a few minutes. He went back after his horse. Hide in the brush there; he'll be back. Give me a gun, Marshal. I'll help —"

"You'll help hell," the marshal said in disgust. "Hey, Joel, fetch up a canteen."

"Listen, Marshal, he jumped us without giving us a chance."

"Oh shut up, El." Cliff looked over where his companions were fighting clear of the last brush pile. "Over here, boys. Now we've got to ride this one back double, as hot as it is."

"He'll be back," El insisted. "He just went after his horse."

Cliff studied the shimmering land for a long time without speaking. Joel Partin knelt and gave El a long pull from a canteen. When he got up the marshal said, "Let's head back. Come on, I'll give you a hand with him, Joel."

When they were assisting El Marlow to stand he kept protesting they should await Ben's return. Finally the marshal swore feelingly and told him, "Listen, you simpleton, Roan's a mile away by now and still travelling. Anyone who'd hunt down four men isn't childish enough to ride into a trap like this. Now keep still; you're going to need all the guts you got before we get you to the doctor."

Thompson was partly right; Ben had withdrawn as soon as he saw Thompson talking to Marlow. He rode back westerly until he cut the trail of Thompson's posse. There he sat in silence for a while, frowning. Finally, he looked at the lowering sun, guessed the time and set a course for Deming.

He followed the posse at a discreet distance until their pace, necessarily slowed by having to ride-double with the wounded man, aggravated him, then he loped out around them and arrived back in Deming an hour and a half before Cliff Thompson entered town at the head of his riders. By then it was dusk.

Ben was slouching on the liverybarn bench, hat back and legs thrust out, when Thompson saw him, cast him a meaningful look, handed his reins to the hostler and stalked over to drop down beside him. Before he spoke to Ben he called out: "Joel, take El to the doctor, then turn him over to Jake Gibbel to be locked up."

The wounded man was glaze-eyed and wilted. He made no protest when Partin took his arm and guided him out into the roadway.

"All right, Ben," the marshal said tiredly. "You can quit acting like you've been here all afternoon."

Ben held out his tobacco sack. When

Thompson took it he straightened up on the bench. Ben watched him work at the paper while he spoke. "I got here over an hour ago. My horse is all cooled-out, too."

"What of it?" Thompson asked, handing the sack back and lighting the cigarette.

"Nothing," Ben replied, "except that I made better time than your posse did."

"Yeah, thanks to you and your carbine."

"What was I supposed to do; let them shoot me?"

"Them?"

"El and Jake Rockwell. He was up there with El until someone got hit, then he lit out."

"For where?"

"Well, that's a tom-fool question. If I knew, I'd be on my way there, instead of sitting around here."

"Now listen, Ben; I asked you not to start any fights."

"I didn't start it. I rode up on them on the mesa and called out. They fired first. After that it was hide-and-seek in that damned brush until El got hit."

Marshal Thompson leaned back, sighed, and rubbed his right leg, which he had bruised on a rock while climbing the knoll. "Did you see old Will and the other one?"

"Nope. All I saw was those two — and a

horse tied in the trees west of the mesa."

"A horse? You mean unsaddled?"

Ben nodded. "Tied there for Rockwell to use after he'd gunned me."

" 'Marlows put it there?"

"I didn't ask El, but I know they did."

"How do you know?"

"Sarahlee told me they were going to."

"I see. Then, that means they were planning on gunning you today."

"Probably. The fact that I got El and scared Rockwell off might have spoilt things for them, but I wouldn't want to bet on it, Cliff. My guess is that Rockwell met Will and Harold, told them about El, and all three of them are riding for Deming right now." Ben craned his neck towards the sky. "This is the third night of the full moon, Cliff; it won't be up until about nine o'clock. A good, dark night for bushwhacking."

"By golly," the marshal said, getting heavily to his feet, "there won't be any of that kind of monkey business in town, while I'm around."

Ben also arose. "Y'know," he said dryly, "for some darned reason I hope you're right. It's pretty hard to see a target at night, especially one that doesn't want to be seen."

"You go on up to your room and stay there."

"I'd figured on doing that, Marshal."

"And I mean *stay there,* too!"

Ben stretched and yawned. "Well, now, you're forgetting something, aren't you?"

"Like what?"

"Sarahlee. She hasn't had supper yet, and neither have I."

"You could have it brought up."

Ben started towards the roadway beyond the barn's darkening maw. " 'Wouldn't look right, Marshal," he said. "But right after we eat, I'll send her home and hibernate."

Marshal Thompson waited until Ben had crossed the roadway and disappeared in the narrow opening of the Oases Hotel's stairway, then he struck out for his office. He was almost to it when Charley Bell hailed him, crossed the road in a trot, and stopped, his face bright with excitement.

"I heard you got Elbert?"

"Well, you heard wrong. Roan shot him and I came up afterwards."

"I see. Did you serve the restraining order I gave you on the other Marlows?"

Marshal Thompson regarded the attorney in stony silence for a moment, then he said, "Oh hell, what's the use," and shouldered past Bell. The lawyer looked after him in bewilderment, then re-crossed the road and started for the hotel stairway.

121

CHAPTER SIX

Sarahlee heard Ben out in silence, then went to the dresser, gazed at herself in the mirror there, and smoothed her hair. When she turned her eyes were shades darker and the fullness of her mouth was relaxed. "I realise from the way you told it, that you could've killed him. Ben, I'm grateful to you."

"How grateful?" He asked, standing in the middle of the room looking at her.

"As grateful as you want me to be."

A loud knock on the door made them both start. Ben asked who it was. When Bell stated his name, Ben let him in. At first the attorney did not see Sarahlee. He was midway through a sentence when he saw her; the words dwindled and died and Bell blinked and flushed.

"I — uh — I . . . Aren't you one of the Marlows, young lady?"

"I am."

Bell's gaze wavered. "Well . . ." he said

lamely. "I thought you were. I recall seeing you before." His eyes went to Ben's face and stayed there. "I just saw the marshal."

"And?"

Bell made a small, deprecatory gesture. "Nothing; nothing important, really."

"He told you about the fight?"

"Not exactly. In fact, I got the impression he didn't want to talk about it."

"That's not very neighbourly, is it? What is it you want to know, Mr. Bell?"

"Oh, nothing. Well, I'm glad it ended like it did, of course. Now I'd better be getting along home. Don't want to be late for supper." Bell went to the door and looked back. "Tomorrow, Mr. Roan; tomorrow's our day in court."

"Fine," Ben said, closed the door after Bell and laughed silently.

"Is he your attorney?"

Ben nodded. "Yes. You sure shook him; I thought he was going to faint when he turned and saw you standing there."

"I nearly fainted myself," Sarahlee said. "Do you know him very well?"

"No, not very well. I know he's pretty busy doing other people's thinking for them, though."

"Charley Bell," Sarahlee said flatly, "is the worst gossip in Deming. That's what I meant when I said I could have fainted when I saw who it was at the door. By tomorrow morning everyone in town will know that I was in your room with you, alone."

"Not tomorrow," Ben said. "He'll be in court."

"He'll find the time, somehow," Sarahlee said wryly, going towards the door.

"Wait, you can't go now. We've got to have supper first."

"I've already eaten. I ate an hour ago, while I was waiting." The way Ben's face fell made some of her tiredness vanish long enough for a faint smile to show through.

"You're not showing much gratitude," he said.

She went deliberately towards him. "No?" she said. "Will this help any?" Her mouth closed down over his and her breath broke against his face, and when he would have put his arms up, she stepped back. There was high colour in her face. "Well . . . ?"

"Yes'm. It helps." He could feel the redness mount in his face but he did not take his eyes off her. "I wish —"

"Good night, Ben, and — thanks."

He remained rooted even after she'd gone, then he roused himself, went to the dresser, washed in the basin there, got his hat and went back downstairs. The first thing he noticed was the slouched figure near the hotel's entrance, holding a shotgun in his arms. He cast a hard look at the man, failed to recognise him, and passed on by heading for the diner. He was straddling the bench in front of the counter before he noticed the lanky cowboy farther down the bench, who also had a shotgun beside him. Later, after his meal had arrived and he was eating, Cliff Thompson came in. He signalled for coffee, sat down beside Ben and looked morosely at Roan's plate of food.

"Where's Sarahlee?"

"She went home."

"Was she upset about the fight?"

"No; she was glad her cousin didn't get killed, is about all. Say; did you send Bell up to my room?"

"Nope. I met him on my way to the office. He started some of that foolish cackle of his and I just walked away. What about him?"

"Nothing. Is he a gossip?"

"One of the best," the marshal said matter-of-factly. "The law business is usually pretty dull around here. Charley's one of those fellers who's born to talk. If he can't do it in court, why then, he just does it anywhere folk'll listen to him."

Ben pushed the plate away and drew his coffee cup closer. "Why all the guards?" he asked, nodding towards the cowboy.

"Like I said, no trouble in town while I'm around."

"Any sign of them?"

"No, and that's what's making me lose sleep. By my figuring they should've ridden into town by now."

Ben looked at Thompson sharply. "You're not that childish, are you? They won't come down the main stem."

"No, I'm not that childish. I've got men all over town. Even in the alleys." The marshal sighed. "If they don't shoot the Marlows they'll probably shoot one another. Just the same, this'd be a poor night to start a fight in Deming."

"You could rely on the court, like Bell does."

Thompson scowled. "Do you?" he said flatly.

Ben got up. "Yeah. I rely on Judge Colt and his six jurymen." He put some coins on the counter and left the café. Outside, night was down in full blackness. He made a cigarette with his back to the café wall, lit it and stood still, smoking, and glinting at the shadows. Satisfied at last, he moved from beneath the overhang, stepped down into the roadway's dust and began angling towards the liverybarn. He was half-way across the road when a sixth sense inside him began to cry a warning. His stride didn't alter but his head went up, rolling from side to side. The acute awareness which preceded every gun-fight sharpened his vision, made him breathe deeper, made him aware of the muscles moving his legs; the muscles filled with the strength of living — of wanting to go on living.

He was almost to the opposite plankwalk when he saw a rusty shadow detach itself from the gloom and start towards him down the road; saw the even tempo of the man's movement, the gentle, cadenced, measured sway of the man's arms and shoulders, as though he was poised for instant action, even while moving. Then he heard the soft call; heard in its faintness the cold challenge.

"*Roan!*"

Everything was there; Ben had been through it before and everything was falling into place. It was always the same. The slurred sound of a name softly called. The cadence of a walking man, the swaying vision of shoulders, of arms out a little from the body, of a head thrown up and of eyes boring in; prelude to a gunfight; to a killing;

sometimes, if the gunmen were close enough, to two killings.

Ben came around slowly. His eyes widened to take in the whole figure up the road, that was slowing now. By the time the killer stopped Ben could see the gun riding low and forward in its russet holster. He could make out the flat planes of cheekbones, the sunken sockets of eyes, the thin lip-line. And he knew this pattern very well. Rockwell was making no secret of his intentions on purpose; he wanted the people of Deming to see him; to notice how he warned Roan; how he fought fair — because there was no aftermath to a fair fight. He would be questioned, maybe cursed; then he would collect his money and ride on.

"Roan."

"That's far enough, Rockwell. Right where you are."

Shadows moved in the darkness on the plankwalk. Into the hush came some soft voices. Someone said: "Go for the marshal," but no one moved to cross the road where the two men stood.

Rockwell said, "You had that kid killed deliberately, Roan. That was a lousy thing to do."

Ben didn't move; he was conscious of what Rockwell had said, exactly as he knew

128

why he had said it: to justify himself; to make it clear to the spectators that Jake Rockwell was killing to revenge a slain youth, which was justifiable.

"Only a coward would have done that, Roan. Have that kid cut down in his own house."

"I had nothing to do with Guy Marlow's killing and you know it, Rockwell."

"You're a liar," Rockwell replied, and turned to stone in the murky light of the roadway.

A cluster of men in front of the Oases Saloon grew as patrons came through the doors. One, drunker than the others, said, "Chriz', how c'they see to shoot?" A clearer voice said, "Shut up."

"You're the same as a murderer, Roan."

Ben said, *"Now!"* and his fingers blurred with movement. In the fraction of a second before the night burst with sound and a lashing of pale flame, a voice down by the café yelled, "Hold it!" But no one heard Marshal Thompson.

Rockwell's gun continued to rise after Ben had fired. It got nearly high enough, then stopped with the barrel pointing downward. When it exploded a large gout of dust blew upwards ten feet in front of Rockwell. His knees bent and he slid down into the roadway and never moved again.

It was ages before Cliff Thompson came up. He passed Ben and knelt by the body in the dust, rolled it over, bent low to squint at the hole in the centre of Rockwell's shirt, then got up and dusted off his knees.

Voices began to rise now, and the drunk at the Oases kept asking who was dead, until someone shut him up. Thompson elbowed around the men who were coming up for a glimpse at the corpse. When he stopped, Ben looked at him over the edge of a cigarette he was making. Neither of them spoke. Thompson finally shrugged his shoulders and asked for Ben's tobacco sack. While he, too, was making a cigarette, he said, " 'Hit you?"

"No, it went into the ground in front of him."

"Good shooting."

"Necessary shooting," Ben said, holding the match. "Where are the other two?"

"I don't know. I didn't know this one was around until someone came bursting into the diner. By then it was too late."

"Yeah. I heard you call out, though."

"I should've kept still."

"It made no difference."

"No . . ."

"Well?"

"Nothing," Thompson said, studying Ben. "He called you; you defended yourself." After a moment's silence the marshal continued: "You're fast, Ben. I'd heard that you were. But, you beat him by a full half-second."

"Anyway, he's dead," Ben said quietly. "And right now that's the important thing."

"One of the important things." Marshal Thompson took Ben's arm and started down the roadway with him. "There's something else that's important, too — only I can't figure it out."

They went into the liverybarn. The marshal halted and pointed to the lined-up rigs under a coal-oil lantern. "That," he said. "That yellow-wheeled buggy there."

Ben went forward, examined the buggy, then turned with a question framed in a frown on his face. "I thought she drove it home?"

"Yeah, that's what I thought, too. I met her on her way out of town." He went closer, stood in front of the rig Sarahlee had driven, and scowled at it. "It looks like she never left town, doesn't it?"

"Maybe she decided it was too late, and got a room for the night."

"Nope, I checked on that before I met you at the diner. I was going to tell you about it, when you walked out. Thompson wheeled and started across the barn to the row of tie-stalls. "Come here," he said, stopping by one stall. " 'You recognise that horse?"

"Sure, that's the blazed-face critter she drove to the buggy."

"Feel him; he's dry as a bone. He hasn't been out of town today."

Ben felt the horse and his brows lowered. "What does it mean, Marshal?"

"I wish I knew, but it looks to me like maybe her kinsmen know about you two. And if they do — and if they've got her — I wouldn't want to be in her boots after what's happened to the Marlows today."

"But, she's a woman."

"One long look'd pretty well convince a man of that all right, but maybe old Will wouldn't notice it, in his present state of mind, Ben. He's had one son killed and for all he knows, the other one could be dead, too. The thing I wish I knew, is whether Will knows she's been talking to you. If I knew that, I'd know what her chances are."

"She's got to be in town somewhere."

"More than likely," the marshal conceded, "but they could've taken her to the ranch, too. Being shy a saddle-horse wouldn't slow them much."

"No, they're around Deming. They

wouldn't walk off and miss my killing."

"That's probably right." The marshal turned towards the opening into the roadway. "I'd give a good horse to know whether they think she told you about Rockwell or not."

"You told me about Rockwell."

Thompson turned, gazed at Ben and shook his head. "All I told you was *who* he was. The rest of it that you knew — you picked up somewhere else. I can guess where; what's troubling me is whether Hal and Will can also guess where."

"Where are you going?"

"To round up a posse and send them up to the Marlow place. Meet me at my office in fifteen minutes. You and I'll search Deming."

After the marshal was gone Ben went up where the nighthawk was standing diffidently, watching him. He was an old man with seamed skin and wet eyes. "I seen the fight," he said tentatively, when Ben stopped beside him. "Pretty dark f'shootin', warn't it?"

"It was pretty dark, yes. Who brought that yellow-wheeled top-buggy in here?"

"Young feller 'bout your age an' size."

"Did you know him?" When the hostler nodded his head but did not reply, Ben said,

"Harold Marlow?"

"Mister," the old man said, "I don't want to get in no trouble."

"You won't, I promise you. Was it Harold Marlow?"

"Yes, 'twas."

"Was Will Marlow with him?"

"No, he brang it in by hisself, and it was empty when he come in with it. I heard you'n Marshal Thompson talkin' back there — but 'twasn't no lady in that buggy when it come in here, I know that for a fact."

"When did Harold bring it in?"

"Mebbe ten, fifteen minutes before the fight."

"What did he say to you?"

"Nothing; just give it to me and walked out. From the black look on his face I didn't feel like askin' no questions, neither."

"Thanks."

Ben handed the nighthawk a coin and walked out into the fresh moon-wash. Little groups of people were talking here and there; as he passed south towards Thompson's office, they watched him go. Jake Rockwell's body was gone from the roadway, and anglingly across from where it had lain, the Oases Saloon's pianist was belting out a tune called "Lorena". Down at the marshal's office horsemen were assembling.

They looked down on Ben as he passed them, bound for the interior of the building. None of them spoke to him. Cliff Thompson waved him to a chair against a cracked, earthen wall, and went outside to give the posse instructions. When he returned with the sounds of their passage backgrounding his words, he said, "Take a shotgun from the rack behind you. I'll finish writing the possemen's names down so's they'll get paid." After hunching over his desk for a while, the marshal threw down a pencil, flexed his fingers and got up. "I don't like to do this, Ben. Maybe if we left 'em alone they'd just ride out peaceable-like."

"Maybe they would — but what about *her?*"

"Yeah. Well, let's go."

"Just a minute, Marshal. I want something understood. If they've done anything to —"

"Aw now, Ben; she's their own flesh and blood."

"You said yourself they might not think of that tonight."

"Well, I know, but after all, the Marlows aren't red-skins."

"If we had the time I'd argue that with you. The point is, Marshal, I've done just about everything you've asked me to do. I've even ridden along with Charley Bell.

Now I want you to understand I'm going to shoot to kill and no questions asked."

"I know how you feel, but let's make sure we've guessed right about this, first. Hell, for all we know Sarahlee could've — well — could've made a dry-camp some place; or maybe be spending the night with friends."

"Yeah? How come Harold took the buggy to the barn, then?"

Thompson got a shotgun from the rack, broke it and plugged shells into it in silence, then he said, "Yeah, I expect that doesn't make much sense, the way I said it. Only, I'd like to keep the killings down to a minimum. After all, the circuit judge'll be here tomorrow. It'll look bad if I've got a cord of corpses for him." He closed the gun with an upward flip. "As a matter of fact, it might not look good, me siding with you."

"I didn't know you were."

"Well, what's it look like right now — you and me going through town together with shotguns?"

"We're not going together. I'll start at the north end of town on the west side of the road, and you start on the other side, from the south end of town."

"Oh no," the marshal said swiftly. "We're going side by side or we're not going at all. If there's another fight I want to be right there among 'em."

They went outside, saw the same little cliques watching them, and started south. When they came to the first cross-road, the marshal nudged Ben. "Might as well start down there."

They went to the last house first, and worked their way gradually along the little street until they were outside the residence of Charley Bell. Cliff started past saying, "What's the use? He won't know anything and he'll keep us there talking for an hour."

"Every house," Ben said stubbornly. "Come on."

Bell met them at the door with a worried expression. When he asked them in, Ben declined, asking if Bell had heard anything about the Marlows or their niece. The lawyer shook his head abruptly. "No, of course not. What's got me worried is Della; she's not home yet and it's almost nine o'clock."

"Where did she go?" Thompson asked.

Bell's expression deepened. "I don't know. It isn't like her to stay out like this. Not at all like her."

"Wait a minute," Ben said softly, turning to Thompson. "You don't suppose they took *both* of them, do you?"

The marshal blinked at him, then looked

at Bell. "Have you any idea when she went out, or why?"

"None at all. When I came home she wasn't here. I figured she'd been to the mercantile, maybe for tinned goods, and had stopped at some friend's place on the way back."

"Well, that's likely, isn't it?"

Bell shook his head. "I just got back from looking for her. She isn't at any of the places I went."

"This is getting too deep for me," Thompson said resignedly. "All right, Mr. Bell, when she shows up let me know, will you?"

"Yes, but supposing she doesn't show up? Supposing something's happened to her, Marshal?"

"Nothing's happened to her. She'll be along. Just let me know as soon as she gets home. I'll ask around for her, so quit worrying."

When they were back down in the roadway, Ben said, "Why her? Not because she's my lawyer's daughter, surely."

"Who can tell? Come on; I want some answers."

They continued to canvass townsmen, their homes, business establishments, and wound up in front of the Oases. Just as they started forward, a frightened, squeaky voice called them furtively from a nearby dog-trot between two buildings. It was the nighthawk from the liverybarn. As soon as they were in the darkness near him, the old man said, "He come an' took the rig. The yellow-wheeled one."

"Harold?"

"Yeh, he was in town all the time. Probably seen the fight. Mebbe was waitin' for a shot hisself, an' never got it, so he's went off somewheres."

"Was he alone?" Ben asked.

The hostler nodded. "He was alone, yeh; but not for long. He had a saddled horse tied to the back of the buggy when he went out of town."

"You saw it?"

"Sure I seen it. 'Else how could I tell you about it."

Ben fished out another coin and put it into the old man's hand. He jerked his head at Marshal Thompson. "We can do our own saddling up. Let's go."

They got their horses and were riding north out of town before the hostler returned from spending his coin at the Oases.

"The Old Man was waiting with the girls. They can't be far ahead," Ben said, lifting his chestnut into a long lope.

Marshal Thompson rode along, riot-gun

balanced across his lap, saying nothing. When they got to the little rise where the scraggly oak-clump stood aloofly to one side, he drew ahead, got down, knelt, and skylined the road. When he got up he grunted and pointed ahead. "About a mile on," he said.

They pushed their horses hard. The land to the north was shadowed by mountains, and although once, when they reined up listening, they heard the buggy, they didn't get close to it until the ruts were curling upward into the trees. Ben hooked the chestnut for an extra burst of speed; he got it, spurted ahead of Marshal Thompson, and drew up within gun-shot of the buggy. When he called out for the driver to pull up, someone pushed a six-gun through the rear curtain and fired at him. The bullet passed overhead but Ben ducked low and his mount shied from the muzzle-blast, a dagger of orange in the night.

Marshal Thompson whipped past. He yelled something which Ben did not hear. The buggy was careening over the ruts; once it struck a rock and bounced high into the air. Thompson had his gun up and cocked. His finger was curling back against the trigger when a scream floated back to him: a woman's cry. He held the gun out briefly;

then let it sag.

Ben's chestnut was fast. As it closed the distance between them, Cliff turned his head. "Don't shoot; she's in the buggy," he yelled over the sounds of the chase. Ben signalled understanding, hooked the chestnut hard, and swung wide. He was trying to get to the trees ahead of the rig, and he might have made it except that the buggy, slewing wildly, struck a stump near the last opening in the road, tilted far up, hung there a moment with black dust quivering up around it, then it went over on its side. The shafts popped like a pistol-shot and the harness-horse staggered, fell, scrambled to his feet and, freed of the rig, fled up the road in panic, dragging the traces, and one piece of a shaft, through the dirt.

Marshal Thompson was closest when the buggy went over. He had seen it going, had reined up swiftly to avoid a collision, and before his horse had set-up, he left the saddle in a run.

Ben, farther out, swung around in a dust-spewing dip that let one stirrup drag the ground a moment, then he, too, left the saddle in a leap and ran towards the up-turned rig.

Two yellow wheels spun in tractionless freedom. From somewhere inside the rig a soft moan came to the running men. Ben, coming in from an angle, was first around in front. He stooped hastily, scooped up something and flung it out into the darkness. Then he holstered his pistol, grabbed an arm and tugged. The man's inert body was heavy. It slid over the dead grass like a wet sack of meal. When Thompson came up he bent forward and squinted.

"It's Hal," he said. "See how he is. I'll get Sarahlee."

Ben looked anxiously at the buggy, saw Thompson's bulk darken the side as he bent over, then Harold Marlow groaned and Ben knelt, ran a hand inside his coat, found a little derringer which he appropriated, then rolled the injured man over onto his back and studied him closely. There was no blood and, as far as he could tell, no broken bones. He felt Marlow's head; there was a pulpy lump coming up behind his right ear. Ben got to his feet and started forward.

The marshal had the girl laid out in the grass. He was kneeling beside her with a puzzled expression, hat far back on his head and a lock of hair curling down across his wrinkled forehead. When Ben came up behind him, the marshal got heavily to his feet.

"How is she?" Ben asked in a rush of words.

"About half knocked-out, is all," Thompson replied slowly, his broad back blocking Ben's view. "Nothing serious." He turned to look at Ben. "How's *he?*"

"Unconscious but otherwise all right, I guess."

"It's Harold, isn't it?"

"Yeah," Ben said, moving around the lawman and kneeling. For a moment he sat on his haunches staring at the girl, then he puckered up his face and looked up. Thompson inclined his head slightly.

"Yeah, sort of took the wind out of me, too."

"But . . . I don't understand. What's *she* doing here?"

Thompson shook his head, watching moonlight play across the girl's white face. "Damned if I know," he said. "Give me your tobacco sack. Might as well smoke while we're waiting for them to come 'round."

Ben handed up the sack and continued to stare at the girl. When she moaned, he bent forward, picked her up by the shoulders and propped her against his leg, and smoothed hair from her face. Thompson lit his cigarette, hunkered down, exhaled, and said, "Della? What in tarnation're you doing out here with Hal Marlow?"

Bedelia Bell's eyes cleared slowly. She looked at Ben and the marshal, and beyond them where Harold lay. She put a hand to her mouth and strained to rise. Ben put a hand on her shoulder and held her down.

"He's all right; just knocked-out is all."

CHAPTER SEVEN

When Charley Bell's daughter recovered, Ben and the marshal set the buggy upright and helped her up into it, then they both stood there waiting. Della kept looking beyond them to where Harold Marlow lay, flat and limp in the moonlight.

"Why doesn't he move?" she asked.

Ben replied, "He got a pretty good knock on the head, ma'm, but he'll come around in a little while. Tell us what you were doing with him? Did he force you to come along?"

The beautiful eyes dropped to Ben's face. "Forced me? Of course not. He's my husband."

Marshal Thompson's cigarette sagged between his lips. "Your what?"

"My husband. We were married two weeks ago over at Las Crucas."

"Well . . ." the marshal said, and halted to reframe his words. "Does your paw know?"

Della shook her head. "No; we decided

not to tell him for a while. You see, he's never cared much for the Marlows. He doesn't know Harold; he doesn't understand how different he is from the others."

"Yeah," Ben Roan said dryly. "He's different all right. Tell me something, Miss Della, where's old Will and Sarahlee Marlow?"

"I don't know. They left us back in town."

Marshal Thompson hooked one booted foot over a broken shaft and gazed at the girl critically. "Della, you marrying *him* is your business. What I want to know is whether you knew Rockwell was in town to kill Roan or not?"

"I — we knew it. I — Harold didn't tell me until I met him in the alley behind my father's house. I tried to talk him out of it, but he told me about El being in jail and badly shot up, and, well, I didn't say anything more against it. I couldn't have reasoned with him anyway, Marshal. He wasn't at all like himself."

"I reckon he wasn't. Where was he hiding when Rockwell met Roan?"

Della's hands fluttered in her lap; she looked down at them. "I'm not sure. When he left me he said for me to meet him at the trough near the north end of town and we'd go to the ranch together."

"Did he mention his paw or his cousin?"

"No."

Ben looked around at the sound of a groan. Hal Marlow was struggling to get up. Ben went over and helped him. As soon as the injured man recognised Ben he jerked his arm away.

"Where's Sarahlee?" Ben demanded.

"I don't know. How's Della?"

"All right; she's in the buggy. Where's the Old Man?"

"I don't know that either. Why don't you go hunt him up. He'd like to see you, Roan."

"I'd like to see him. Why did he take Sarahlee with him?"

"You know the answer to that; why ask me? She's been carryin' tales to you. She put you onto Rockwell; she set you onto El; she's turned as treacherous as an Injun and I think the Old Man figures to kill her for that. One thing, Roan — Marlows stick together. They don't tolerate any treachery."

Ben looked at Marlow very steadily. "That's been working both ways, Hal. There's only one way you knew about Sarahlee and me," Ben nodded towards the buggy. "Della told you; she heard it from her paw and told you. The difference is, I don't hold it against her. I was raised to believe loyalty comes from the heart, not from a name." He took Marlow's arm and shoved him over by the buggy. Della spoke to Harold; he answered with a short grumble and felt his head gingerly.

Marshal Thompson was listening to something with his head cocked to one side. When he was satisfied with what he heard he faced Marlow. "Good thing you didn't get up there, Hal. That's a posse comin' down the road. They might've done more than upset your buggy."

"Like they did to Guy!"

Thompson looked at his captive a long moment before he said, "There's nothing I can do about that now, beyond sayin' I'm real sorry. He didn't give us much choice, Harold; the second we rode into the yard he opened up on us."

"And El?"

"The marshal wasn't in on that until it was all over," Ben said shortly. "El and Rockwell fired first. After El was hit Rockwell skinned out."

"I wish he'd killed you, Roan."

"I expect you do. No thanks to any of you that he didn't," Ben replied. "If he'd fought like you fellows fight he probably could have, too."

Hal Marlow's eyes pinched down tight. "You think we fight from cover, do you; just let me have a gun and I'll show you here and now, by God!"

"Harold!" Della's hand reached out to touch her husband's arm. He shook it off.

"How about it, Roan? You man enough or not?"

"None of that," the marshal said harshly. "In the first place he'd kill you, Hal; in the second place you're going to jail in one piece."

The possemen jogged up to the buggy and hauled up. Marshal Thompson waved his hand at the broken shafts and said, " 'Couple you boys give me your lass ropes." He worked to free the remains of the shafts, tied the ropes to the axle and ran them out to their owners. "Dally 'em," he said, "and pull the thing back to town." Turning back, he waved a hand at Della. "You can ride with her, Hal, or you can ride double with me. Let's get going."

Harold got in beside his wife. Ben caught his horse, mounted, watched the riders turn the buggy and start back towards Deming with it. He heard fragments of a conversation between Marshal Thompson and one of the possemen. They hadn't found anyone at the Marlow place.

The ride back was accomplished without much talk. The buggy was left at the livery-barn and Ben followed the marshal and his prisoners to the office. After the posse was dismissed and only the four of them were in the room, Ben confronted Harold with a steady eye and a hard expression.

"Where did he take her?" he demanded.

Harold shrugged, turned towards the bench and would have sat down, but Ben caught his arm, whirled him around and grabbed the front of his shirt. *"Where!"*

Della looked from Ben's darkening face to Marshal Thompson. Her husband struggled in Ben's grip. "Stop them," the girl said. Marshal Thompson looked at her, shrugged, and sat down behind his desk.

"It's not my fight," he said.

"But it's — it's — assault; bodily assault."

"Not from where I'm sitting, ma'm. No one's been hit yet." He swung his eyes to Marlow's face. "You'd better tell him, Hal."

"I don't know!"

Ben's grip tightened. When Marlow brought up a fist Ben knocked it aside. "I want the truth, Hal. Where did he take her?"

"I don't know — and that's the absolute truth."

Ben flung him back towards the bench. "Where did you see them last?"

"At the edge of town. I had Rockwell's horse with me. I gave it to him. He put Sarahlee on it. He rode his own horse and was leading mine. They went north-west. That's all I can tell you."

"What did he do to her?"

"Called her some names — that's all."

Thompson put his hands behind his head and leaned back in the chair. "Where would he be likely to take her, Hal?" he asked. "Now, you know old Will better'n any of us. You've got a notion where he'd take her."

"All I know is that my uncle's coming up from Santa Fe on the morning coach. Paw might've taken her down the trail to meet him — to give her to her paw and tell him what she did to us."

Thompson's chair creaked as he swung forward and arose. "Why didn't I think of that. Jake Gibbel told me her paw was coming to Deming."

"And if he didn't take her down the trail to meet him," Ben said, "what then? We'll have ridden a long way for nothing, and he'll still have her."

Thompson considered this for a moment, then he gazed at Della. "You go on home," he said. "Your paw's worried about you. And you stay there, too. If I see you on the street again I'm going to arrest you."

"What grounds could you arrest her on?" Marlow demanded.

"Aiding fugitives'll do for now," the marshal said, scooping up a ring of keys from the desk. "Come on, Hal, you've been worrying about El. I'll put you in the same cell with him."

When Cliff returned from locking up the second Marlow, Ben Roan was standing in the middle of the office frowning at the floor. He looked up and said, "Marshal, you go after the stage. I'm going up in the hills."

"You think he took her up there?"

"I don't know, but there's no point in both of us riding in the same direction, is there?"

"I guess not. Y'know, Ben, old Will's stuck his leg in the bear-trap this time. Bad enough he's taken his brother's daughter against her will, but there's a law against abduction, and that makes him a fugitive for sure."

"I don't give a damn about your law," Ben shot back. "I want Sarahlee back unhurt."

"You'll get her that way. You heard what El said. The Old Man cussed her out."

"I don't believe Hal."

They went back out into the night. Deming was going to bed. Even the hilarity at the Oases was lessening. They got horses at the liverybarn and parted in the roadway. The last thing Marshal Thompson said was, "Ben, I want you to bring him in alive if it's at all possible, and I want your word you'll

152

try to do it."

"You've got it," Ben replied, and reined north out of town. As soon as he was clear of the last buildings, he cut easterly, and the silver light of a nearly-full moon made it easy for him to see.

He rode at first to the Marlow place, not believing he would find anyone there, but confident that he would find that Will Marlow had been there, because, unlike Marshal Thompson, he had not forgotten the old grandfather, who would be alone at the ranch now, and being infirm, would need attention. Nor was he wrong. The old man was inside the house, wrapped in a blanket and propped up in a chair. A partially consumed bowl of porridge was on a table nearby and when Ben put his hand against it, the bowl was still warm. He drew up a chair and said, "Mr. Marlow — do you remember Ben Roan?"

"Eh?"

"Ben Roan. Benjamin Roan . . ."

"Ben? Ben . . . it's been a long time. They tol' me ye died . . . They tell me lots o' things, Ben. 'Tell me they own your place on the creek now . . . Ben; I don't see good no more . . ." The old man's eyes didn't focus and dampness lay in the creased flesh below them. "How's Ellie, Ben . . . How's the boy?"

"Fine, Eph," Ben said, "fine. Where's Will and his boys?"

" 'Round somewheres, Ben. 'Round somewheres . . . Cal's girl's here now, too. You never met her, did you Ben?"

"No, I never did," Ben said, feeling strange, acting the part of his own father; feeling the tug of years drawing him back to a time when he remembered this senile old man as different.

"Fine big girl, Ben. Saraylee they call her. Fine girl. Make a good woman f'that boy of your'n, come a few years for 'em to sprout up in. Don't look like Cal much, though."

"Was she just in here, Eph?"

"Yeh; jes' left, Ben. 'You see her? Fine big girl . . ." The old man's eyes wavered, grew misty. "Jim Bridger jes' here, too. Hey, Jim, han' me that jug . . . Jim, consarn ye . . ."

"How long ago was Sarahlee here, Eph?"

"How's that . . . ? Saraylee . . . Bridger. Now you're joshin with me . . . Them Two-Kettles are bad; let me tell ye' boy — shoot first. No matter what the soljers say — shoot first. Ain't that right, Jim? Sure 'tis . . ."

"Eph, can you hear me, Eph? Where did Sarahlee go?"

"Sareylee? Yeh, jes' here."

"With Will?"

"Will? Oh him . . . Well, not like his brother Cal, Jim; not a little bit, nossir. But Cal's —"

Ben stood up, looked down at the old man, at his milky gaze, and walked silently back outside, went around the house looking for tracks. Near the rear of the house he found them. A fresh overlay of horseshoes above the sign left by Thompson's posse. He was bending to look closer when he heard a horse coming in a fast lope. He moved swiftly to the side of the house, unshipped his gun, cocked it and waited.

Marshal Thompson swept into the yard with a riot-gun held high in one fist. Ben stepped out into sight and let the dog down on his pistol. "I thought you were going after the stage, Marshal."

Thompson swung down, head swinging from side to side. "Changed my mind, Ben. Anybody around here?"

"Just the grandfather. He's inside," Ben said, moving out into the yard.

"I was leaving town when a couple of travellers came in. They said they'd seen a man and a girl riding like the devil after a crippled saint, heading north. I figured it'd be the Old Man and Sarahlee."

"I guess it was," Ben said, jerking his head towards the house. "Sarahlee's been here, anyway. She fed her grandpaw some mush. The bowl's still warm."

Cliff looked at the house, let the dogs down on the shotgun and relaxed. "Pick up any sign?"

Ben nodded. "Come around back."

The marshal tied his horse and followed Ben. They were studying the tracks, and Ben was reaching for a match, when a sharp, flat gunshot erupted. Marshal Thompson gave a startled grunt and flung himself sideways, towards the wooden steps leading to the back porch behind them. Ben, moving like lightning, hit the ground in a roll. A burst of flame blossomed from his right fist. He crawled swiftly towards the porch and worked his way under it, into the dank shadows there.

Crouching low beside the steps Marshal Thompson swore savagely. "Where did it come from, Ben?"

"The trees back there."

Stillness settled over the yard. Moonlight shone off a dented can lying out a ways. "What's he waiting for?" Marshal Thompson demanded. "He's got us pinned down here."

"Stick your head up and find out," Ben said, pushing debris aside and lying flat.

"Go to hell."

Ben strained to see beyond the first fringe of bull-pines, their shaggy limbs making deep darkness beyond, where the gunman was. "Toss a rock over there," he said.

The marshal squirmed around to find one, and had no luck. "Aren't any," he said. "If it's Will he just did that to hold us here while he got away."

Ben raised his hand-gun and fired. The echoes rocketed down the night. No answering shot came back.

"He's gone," Thompson said, and began to edge away from the stoop. A shot shattered the steps above the marshal's head. He hunched down close to the ground and swore again.

Ben waited a while, then twisted to look around him. The porch was several feet off the ground. Out towards the front of the house, though, the sloping earth raised upwards; there wasn't room enough between it and the sub-flooring for a man's body to squeeze through. On his right, northerly from the steps, the porch ran out and moonlight showed it to be at least eighteen inches from the ground. He squirmed around, made sure his body could get through, then said in a low voice to the marshal: "I'm going to try to get behind him. If he starts shooting, try to draw his fire."

"All right."

The yard was hushed and opaque in the moonlight. Ben crawled under the porch to its northerly end, and squeezed through. Nearby was racked stove-wood. He inched towards it, watching the trees over his left shoulder. When he was safely hidden from sight he studied the land off to his right, which he would have to cross to reach the forest's fringe. There was a shed of some kind fifty feet away, and nearer, open ground lay bare and sere in the soft light. Beyond the shed some stumps would shield him, but he was certain Marlow would see him as soon as he left the woodpile. He tossed a stone over where the marshal was, and when Thompson's head came around the steps, Ben motioned with his gun towards the trees, and gestured towards the open ground. Thompson drew back, and a moment later he fired two fast shots into the timber. Instantly a carbine sounded and Ben, not waiting to hear the marshal reply, sprinted towards the shed. He made it, flattened against the woodwork and edged along it to the first stump. After that, with the gun feud raging behind him, he made his way into the fringe of trees, turned south and began working his way down towards the spot where the attacker was firing. He was almost there when the firing ceased as suddenly as it had begun, and a strange voice called out: "You there by the porch: throw your gun out and stand up."

Marshal Thompson's answer came back in high anger. "If you want this gun, come out and get it."

"Listen, mister; I can keep you there until daybreak."

"You're wrong," the marshal called back. "But if you were right it wouldn't change anything."

"You've got a minute to make up your mind," the hidden gunman said, "then I'm going to cut you down."

"Hah! You haven't been able to do it so far; another minute isn't going to help you any. Why don't you let Sarahlee come out, so she won't be endangered?"

There was a long silence. Then the attacker said, "What are you talking about?"

Marshal Thompson opened his mouth to reply, heard a sharp exchange of words in among the trees, and called out, "You get him, Ben?"

"I got him, Marshal. Come on over."

"You got his gun?"

"Yes."

The marshal got slowly to his feet, flexed his legs and started across the yard. Just before he got to the trees Ben came out of them driving a thick-set, burly man ahead of him. Thompson stopped short, looked at the stranger and scowled.

"Who the hell are *you?*"

"My name's Marlow. That house you were trying to break into belongs to my brother."

Ben's gun sagged earthward. He went around where moonlight struck the captive's face, and stared. "Marlow?"

"That's right. Calvin Marlow. That is my brother's house there. Who are you two, and what were you doing, skulking around here?"

Marshal Thompson looked at Ben, holstered his pistol and drew back his coat. His silver star in its circlet of steel shone dully. "I'm a U.S. Marshal, mister. This is Ben Roan."

"A marshal . . . ?"

"That's right. Tell me something, Mr. Marlow — what town are you from?"

"Santa Fe. I was on —"

"I thought you weren't going to arrive in Deming until tomorrow?"

"It would've been later than that, Marshal. The stage broke down at a ranch about five miles south of Dueña. I borrowed a horse and rode up here."

"Why didn't you go to Deming first?"

"Why should I? There's nothing in Deming I want to see. I came on up to my brother's place. I'm planning on taking my daughter back to Santa Fe, you see, and —"

"I see all right," Thompson said. "How long were you there in the trees before you opened up on us?"

"I'd just finished tying the horse; was moving towards the yard when I saw you two bending down there."

"You thought we were robbers?"

Calvin Marlow inclined his head. "I knew you weren't my brother or his boys."

"Well —"

"Wait a minute," Ben said, interrupting. "Mister Marlow, when you were riding up, did you see any other riders?"

"Yes, as a matter of fact, I did. Two of them, riding like Indians out that way." Marlow raised an arm and pointed to the east.

"One of them was your daughter, Sarahlee. The other one was your brother, Will."

"What? Why would they be riding like that?"

"I'll get his horse," the marshal said, and

started towards the trees.

Ben led Cal Marlow around to the front of the house and inside where the old man sat. "Who is that?" he asked, pointing towards the bundled figure in the chair.

"Why, that's my father," Marlow said, and moved forward. "Hello, dad. It's me — Cal."

The old eyes lifted and a shaft of sanity shone in their sunken depths. "Cal? Glad you come, boy. 'Been someone out back shootin', see who 'twas, will ye?"

"It's all right now, Dad. Where's Will? What's been happening up here, anyway?"

"Happening . . . ? Why, nothing . . ." The sunken eyes went past Marlow to the opened door, and hung there in a vacant stare. "Coon up that tree, boy . . ."

Marlow turned. "He gets rational spells, but not for long."

"I know," Ben said. "I talked to him a while back and he thought I was my father, who's been dead twenty-four years."

Marshal Thompson came trooping into the room. He studied the older man a while, then said, "Maybe we'd ought to take him back with us, Ben."

"Not ahorseback," Cal Marlow cut in swiftly. "He's too frail."

"All right, I'll send a buggy out. Come on, let's get back to town."

"But —" Marlow began, and the marshal cut him off by turning his back and starting down the steps towards the horses.

Ben said, "We'll tell you about it on the way to town."

By the time they reached Deming, Calvin Marlow had heard of the fight; of how his brother had his daughter, and how his brother's three sons were either in jail or dead. He rode in stunned silence. Not until he was in the marshal's office did he speak.

"Let me see Elbert and Harold."

The two boys were surprised to see their uncle, but refused to answer his questions until Ben took the key from Cliff and inserted it in the lock. Then Elbert said, "All right. There's not much to tell anyway. Paw went wild, Uncle Cal. He didn't act like himself after Guy was killed. Then we heard that Hal was dead, too, and he swore he'd kill everyone who's crossed him."

"But, Elbert — Sarahlee's his own niece, boy."

"I know. I tried to talk sense to him. I told him she'd only slow us down. He said he'd teach her to betray her own flesh and blood."

"Go on."

"There isn't any more. I took my wife and started for the ranch. These two here chased me, and here I am."

"But where did Will go?"

Elbert shook his head. "I don't know, Uncle Cal. He made me light out alone."

"He went east, El, towards the mountains. Where would he be taking her, in that country?"

"I told you; I don't know."

Harold Marlow spoke from the straw pallet where he was reclining on one elbow. "There's six hundred miles of mountains there. Go try and find him."

Ben stood thoughtfully to one side. Now he spoke. "I've got a better idea. You stay here, Mister Marlow. We'll find Sarahlee and your brother and bring them both back here." He walked out into the office and Marshal Thompson trailed after him.

"What's on your mind, Ben?"

"Grandpaw Marlow. As long as Will knows his father's alone at the ranch he'll come back to care for him."

The marshal said, "Of course."

They left the office together. Ben paused long enough to look out over the darkened town. "No chance of getting a posse up, I guess."

"Not at this hour, without ringing the fire-bell. What do we need one for, anyway?"

"To block the trails east from Will's place

into the mountains," Ben replied, then moved towards the hitch-rack. "Well, if we're lucky we won't need to block the trails."

They rode out of town for the second time that night, and they didn't speak for the full distance of the ride until just before sighting the Marlow Ranch. Then Ben said, "For a man who's not supposed to use this cussed road, I've been using it more the past couple of days than I ordinarily would have used it in a month."

"Well, don't crow about it," the marshal said, reining over towards the gate into the yard. "After the judge makes his decision you may never use it again."

Ben got down tiredly, stumped up the steps and stopped. When Cliff got up beside him, he said, "Go on; what're you waiting for?"

Ben jutted his chin out. "That door was open when we left, before."

Thompson stared at the panel and under his breath he said, "Oh no," then flung the door back and stalked into the room. Ben's voice sounded softly from outside.

"Gone, isn't he?"

Marshal Thompson didn't answer. He went through every room in the house before he came back out onto the porch.

Ben was down by the horses, bending forward and using matches to pick up shod-horse sign. The marshal went down towards him. "Don't tell me," he said, "let me guess. They went east."

Ben straightened up and flung the burnt-out match away from him. "He'd like us to think he did. But I'll lay you odds if we lay over here until dawn we'll find that he went east only a little ways, then turned south towards town." He went over to his horse, toed in and sprang up. "He couldn't take that old man up into those hills if he wanted to; the old feller'd fall off a horse, and even if the ride didn't finish him, living off brush-berries and camp-cooked rutting-buck would."

The marshal mounted stiffly and crossed his hands over the saddlehorn, looking up where the moonlight bathed the high, forested peaks. "Y'know, Ben, if Will Marlow was a real fugitive from justice, he couldn't act any worse."

"You said he was a fugitive."

"Well, yes. But you know how that is. If the fool'd just ride in and let Sarahlee go, no one'd say much, least of all me. And you know why? Because I'm running out of whatever it is that keeps a man going hour after hour, day and night."

Ben reined towards the east. "That's just exactly what he's hoping for, Cliff. But we're going to disappoint him. We're going to find his trail and dog it until he's willing to call quits."

They rode in single-file, Ben leading, up through the tiers of trees, and whenever the marshal had doubts, he looked at Ben's back and they disappeared. Ben had a destination in mind and he was making for it with a singleness of purpose that allowed no time for fatigue, nor any thought for peril.

CHAPTER EIGHT

Marshal Thompson was drowsing in the saddle when Ben led the way down through the forest to the juniper-slope above Horse Flat. When his horse stopped, Thompson was jarred awake. He opened his eyes, looked at Ben's back, and beyond where pale silver washed the fifty-acre clearing. He didn't see the horse until Ben twisted, raised his right arm and pointed, then he nudged his mount down beside Ben's horse and leaned forward squinting.

"Is it saddled?"

"Yeah. Let's tie up here."

They went forward afoot, moving carefully through the brush. Finally, Ben stopped and leaned close to the lawman. "Stay here; I'll try to get east of them and cut them off from the mountains. When you hear me call out for Will to throw down his gun, you holler from back here so he'll think it's a posse."

The marshal nodded and said, "Be careful."

Ben moved down through the skirting fringe of brush, and just when he was congratulating himself on the silence of his approach, a low-skimming owl, hunting for mice, swooped too low, saw Ben too late, and beat the air with frantic wings, letting out a frantic scream as it struggled for altitude. Ben crouched, cursed the big bird and watched the place where the saddled horse was. A lean, long-limbed man appeared in the clearing, his carbine held low and ready. Neither he nor Ben moved for a full minute, then the man straightened up gradually, let the gun sag, and turned back to the fringe of brush from which he'd emerged.

Ben continued to work his way closer. Although the moonlight was bright enough in the open, where Ben moved through the copse it was dark and shadowy. He did not realise how much ground he had covered until movement blurred no more than fifty feet in front of him, and a voice said, "Save the rest of it." The answering voice made a thrill pass through him; he'd have known it anywhere.

"He needs it now, Uncle Will."

"I said save it!"

169

"Oh . . . This is insane; it's cruel."

"You made it that way, girl."

"All right, that's all I've heard for hours; he's old, Uncle Will, and he's not strong. You can't just go on —"

"I can! I've got to, d'you hear? He couldn't stay back there — there wasn't anyone to look after him."

"Uncle Will . . . !"

"That's enough Sarahlee. Not another word. Help me get him back on the horse."

"I won't!"

Ben saw the dark, thin shadow straighten up from its crouch over a prostrate form. "You what," Will Marlow said, in a tight, rasping tone. "What did you say — you Jezebel, you; you filthy, rotten traitor, you . . ." Marlow's long arm started to swing upwards.

Ben neither moved nor spoke. He drew his gun and cocked it; the snippet of sound, unmistakable, was loud and deadly in the night. Will Marlow's arm hung in the air, his body seemed turned to stone. Very slowly, without moving the rest of his body, he began to turn, to twist his head to see behind him.

Ben said, "Take his gun, Sarahlee."

"By God you won't get it!" Will Marlow snarled, dropping his arm with the speed of light and whirling.

"You damned fool!" Ben swore. "Don't . . ."

Marlow roared "Hah!" and his fingers closed around the butt of his six-gun. It was moving upwards when Ben fired. Marlow went half around and fell forward into a thicket of buck-brush. Sarahlee screamed, then put both hands over her face and sagged forward. Ben caught her, let her down beside her grandfather, whose eyes were tightly closed and whose pale, wasted face was like parchment in the moonlight.

Marshal Thompson charged through the brush like a maddened bull. When he came up he was hatless and his gun was cocked. He stared at Sarahlee on the ground, at the old man, then looked over where Ben was pulling Will Marlow out of the brush. "Is he dead?" he asked sharply.

"No, but that gun of his won't be worth much."

"You didn't shoot him?"

"Nope; shot his holstered gun; the slug darned near knocked him over backwards."

Marshal Thompson holstered his pistol, helped Ben extricate Will Marlow, then shook the rancher like a dog shakes a rat. "Marlow, you damned idiot, are you all right?"

Marlow glared at them both. "All right? You damned murderers . . . I'll kill you both. I swear it on the Bible; I'll get both of you if it's the last thing I ever do!"

"It just might be the last thing you ever do, if you try it," Thompson said, tightening his grip on Marlow's shoulder. "Ben, see how Sarahlee and the old gaffer are, will you?"

Sarahlee got up slowly, swayed against Ben and buried her face against the front of his shirt. He touched her hair, stroked it clumsily, then held her away from him. "Are you all right? Did he harm you, Sarahlee?"

"No, I'm all right. But Grandpaw . . ."

"Don't worry about him. You and I'll stay here until the marshal sends a buggy back."

Cliff gave Marlow a hard shove out into the clearing towards the horses. "It'll be daybreak or better before anyone can get up here, Ben, but I'll hurry 'em."

"We'll be here," Ben said. "And Marshal, send back some quilts and maybe some milk for the old man."

"Sure."

They watched Thompson take Will Marlow away. For a while neither of them spoke, then Sarahlee knelt beside her grandfather and took one of his hands in both her own hands; without looking around at Ben she

172

said, "I'm glad you didn't shoot him; he isn't himself."

Ben sank down and made a cigarette. "You're the only reason I didn't shoot him. Hal told me that he swore at you for telling me things."

"It doesn't matter, Ben; besides, in a way he was right. I shouldn't have."

He inhaled deeply, looked at her profile in the moonlight, blew the smoke out and turned his head a little, to see the old man. "I expect it was pretty hard on him, wasn't it?"

"It was insane, plain crazy, to even attempt it."

"Where did Will think he was going, with him?"

"He was going to lose you in the mountains, then go down to Deming, get a room at the hotel, and wait for you to ride into town."

"And bushwack me."

"Yes."

Ben continued to gaze at the old man. "Will he be all right?"

"I think so. It's a warm night. He's asleep now." She sat back on her heels and looked across at Ben. "I rode beside him and held him in the saddle. I don't think he even knows he isn't at home."

"Your paw's here, Sarahlee."

She was startled. "Here, in Deming?"

"Yeah. Thompson and I met him at the ranch and took him back to town with us. He's going to take you back to Santa Fe." His glance swept up to her face. "I guess you'll be glad to go, won't you?"

Sarahlee got to her feet and moved over closer, then sank down beside Ben. "Not particularly," she said. "Ben?"

"Yes'm."

"Look at those stars. They're clearer up here than they are in Santa Fe."

"Pretty all right," he replied, looking at her face, at the way her head was tilted back, at the russet sheen of her hair in the moonlight, and at the full sweep of her throat.

"You aren't looking at the stars, Ben."

"I'm looking at you." He squashed the cigarette. "Sarahlee, I'd sure admire to marry you."

Her head came down and around. "Well, why don't you?"

He made an out-flung gesture with his hand. "Because I don't even have a cabin for you to live in, now."

"I could help you build one."

He blinked at her. "At Roan's Creek?"

"I can't think of a lovelier spot, Ben. You

174

know, long before you came back, that was my favourite hideaway. When I wanted to be alone, I'd go up there and sit by the cottonwoods. I even fished the creek a few times."

"Catch anything?" he asked with mock gravity.

"Nothing of any size. Ben?"

"Yes'm."

"Do you know what it takes to get married?"

"I reckon I do. Money, some tools, a few horses and maybe some —"

"All it takes is love."

He looked at the ground for a moment. "Well, I expect that'd do fine for a while," he said, "but I think you'd get mighty tired of a diet of just love after a few years."

She twisted towards him and the moonlight made shadows around and over her, especially under her chin and lower, above the tucked-in flatness of her stomach. "Would you get tired of living on love, after a year or two, Ben?"

He looked at her, and looked quickly away. "No'm," he said softly, "I don't expect I would. But I was thinking of you, not me."

"I wouldn't get tired of it."

"Then I expect the thing for us to do," he said matter-of-factly, "is get married. Do you like any particular day, like maybe this afternoon, or tomorrow. That'd be Thursday, wouldn't it?"

She wrinkled her nose at him. "I can't keep this up like you can," she said. "I'm too — I'm all upset inside." She held her hand out. They watched the quiver of her fingers a moment, then Ben took the hand and drew her to him.

She murmured, "Oh, Ben — I was so frightened."

"I know . . ." He ran his fingers through her hair. "It's all over now, Sarahlee."

"Kiss me, Ben."

He did; he held her lips with his until she put both arms around his neck and drew him tight, and when the strength of her holding became weak and passive, he pulled back.

"I reckon I ought to tell you that I love you, ma'm," he said.

"I reckon you had. It's a mutual feeling. Like I said once before — it's been here inside me for a week, but if I had to explain how it got there, I couldn't. It's just there . . ."

"When I knew Will had you, I felt about like he must've felt after Guy was killed. I wanted to get my hands on him; not shoot him; not go up against him with a gun. I wanted to get my hands around his throat."

"He really wasn't bad to me, Ben. He just wasn't himself. He threatened me, but I wasn't afraid."

"What did the boys do?"

"El didn't say a word, but then El's never really liked me anyway. Hal tried to talk to Uncle Will."

"Did you know Hal was married to Della Bell?"

"Not until they told me. Not until they met us at the edge of town."

"Does Will know?"

She nodded. "He knows. Hal told him when we met after the fight — but I don't think he paid any attention to what Hal was saying." She touched his throat with her fingertips. "Uncle Will made me stand back in the shadows with him and watch the fight. He told me he gave Rockwell one thousand dollars to kill you."

"What did he say afterwards?"

"It wasn't what he said — he swore — it was the way he looked. His face was twisted and hateful looking." Her fingertips went to his breast and lay there feeling the pound of his heart. "I — waited with them. While I was waiting I tried to think of everything I'd ever heard about you as a gunman. I tried to make myself believe you'd come through alive. I even prayed you'd kill Rockwell. When the shooting happened, I closed my eyes and prayed . . . We couldn't be sure who was down because we were too far away. Uncle Will went as far as the plank-walk, but before he came back I knew it was Rockwell because he'd come down from the south and your back was to us. It was still to us after the shooting stopped. I was so thankful I cried. Hal's wife put her arm around my shoulders. Then Uncle Will came back, told Hal to get the buggy and go to the ranch and look after grandpaw until he got up with me."

"The marshal sent a posse up there."

"I know. Uncle Will went around the back way and we sat on the ridge watching. After they left we went down and I fed grandpaw. Then he said we'd better come back later, and we left again." She put her head against him. "I wasn't tired then, Ben, but I am now."

He pushed her back and put his arm under her head. "Rest a little while. I'll watch the old man."

She reached up with both arms and pulled him down. Her mouth sought his and they were close for a long moment, then he lay back beside her and looked up where the tattered sky hung, paling-purple, with light showing through from hundreds of pin-prick holes. Higher in the mountains a wolf howled, a long, rolling tumult of sound that ended in soft echoes.

He was tired clear through but his mind would not rest. His thoughts were a mingling of old, and new; of memories bridged by the years; he could recall with stark reality the times he and his father had been at this same mesa, and in the fullness of the night he could see his father's slow, approving smile. Beside it was Sarahlee's wan face, her anxious look, and closer, the twisted expression of Will Marlow.

Time passed, his arm ached, and the stillness grew thin with the pale pink of pre-dawn. It was warm and pleasant and he finally closed his eyes. It seemed he'd only been asleep a minute or two when someone shook him gently.

"The buggy's here, Ben."

He sat up, rubbed his eyes and felt the scratchiness of his beard. Sarahlee looked fresh. Somehow, she'd combed her hair, and the tiredness was gone from her face, only a hint of shadow lay around her eyes. She smiled at him.

"You slept like a child."

"How's grandpaw?" he asked.

"He seems all right. He awakened a few

minutes ago and asked for breakfast."

Ben ran bent fingers through his hair, clamped his hat on and listened to the bump and grind of an approaching wagon. When he stood up he saw it, winding its way slowly down through the thicket. There were two men on the seat. One he recognised as Joel Partin, the blacksmith. The other man, clasping a dark leather bag on his lap and frowning anxiously as the rig jolted over boulders, spoke sharply to Partin as they broke through the last fringe of copse and turned easterly along the mesa. Partin nodded, threw his head back and called out.

"Over here," Ben replied, pushing out into the open.

When Partin drew up and set the brake, he looked dubiously down at Ben. "Where's the old man?" he asked. "This here's Doc Brundage — Cliff got him to come along."

Ben flagged his arm towards the brush. Brundage got down with an effort and started stiff-legged towards Sarahlee, who was standing in plain sight. Ben helped Partin secure the team, then he looked in the back and Partin, guessing his thoughts, said, "There's milk there, some quilts, an' a pony of whisky."

They waited until the doctor had examined the old man, then made a stretcher of quilts, carried him to the wagon and made him comfortable in the back. Ben helped Sarahlee get in with her grandfather. Doctor Brundage looked squarely at Ben for the first time. He said nothing, but there was interest in his glance. Finally, he motioned for Joel Partin to start back.

Ben got his saddle-horse, tied the lead-rope of Sarahlee's horse into the tail of the beast her grandfather had ridden, then led both horses over the trail behind the wagon, from his saddle.

Joel Partin smarted under the sharp tongue of the doctor every time he hit a boulder or jolted the wagon across a gully. Not until they were back on the Roan Creek road travelling south towards the prairie, did he relax, take a chew from his plug of Kentucky Twist, and look around at Ben.

"Sure's hell to pay in town," he said. "That other Marlow's madder'n a wet hen at old Will. Cliff threatened to put him in jail, too, if he didn't settle down."

"Cliff have any trouble getting Will back?"

"Naw, no trouble. But the old gaffer was fit to be tied. I don't recollect ever seeing him so worked up before, and I've known him quite a spell."

By the time they got to the seepage sump

where Roan Creek petered out, Doctor Brundage said they'd better stop. It was boiling hot by then, so they soaked two of the quilts in the water and erected a makeshift awning over Grandfather Marlow. Joel watered the horses, Brundage squatted by his patient, and Ben smoked a cigarette in the shade. Sarahlee washed her face at the creek, twisted around and called. Ben went forward. She was smiling up at him through the sparkle of creek-water.

"It makes you feel so much better. Try it."

He did; got down on his knees, lay his hat aside and washed his face. The water was as cool as dew. He rubbed it into his skin, trickled it over his head, put his hat back on and grinned. "Washes the meanness out," he said.

"What meanness?"

"Oh, things I've been thinking."

She got up facing him. "It's over now, Ben," she said. "Think of something else. Think of the new cabin up at Roan's Creek."

He got up slowly. "Is that what you've been thinking about?"

"Yes." She started to turn away. "That — and the fact that I'm hungry."

"Maybe this'll hold you until you can get something better," he said, catching her arm, bringing her around slowly, and kissing her full on the mouth.

"That's better than breakfast," she said, when he released her.

They went back to the wagon. Doctor Brundage had his back to them. He and Joel were talking. The blacksmith swung his head at their approach. "Ready to go?" he asked, and when Ben nodded he clambered up onto the wagon-seat.

The day had turned yellow and mistily shimmering by the time they left the creek and travelled south towards Deming. Ben, riding at the tailgate, watched Sarahlee care for her grandfather. When they were still two miles out several riders raised a dust far west of them. It was impossible to make out their numbers, but Ben was satisfied it was more than one horseman.

A mile closer, another body of riders appeared out of the heat making directly for the wagon. Joel Partin called Ben's attention to them. Ben rode on around the wagon, trotted ahead a ways and halted, watching. The horsemen didn't slacken pace. When the wagon came up, Ben waved Partin to a halt.

"Reception committee, more'n likely," Partin said.

Doctor Brundage's nasal voice sounded

irritated. "Don't let them upset the old man. He's had enough excitement." He scowled at the riders. "Roan, ride ahead and tell them we can do without their hurrahing."

But Ben didn't move. Some instinct held him motionless, watching the horsemen swing closer.

"That's Jake in the lead," Partin said suddenly, and most of the casualness went out of his voice. He set the brake, let his booted foot hang on the iron rung, and the lines hung forgotten in his hands. Behind him, Sarahlee stood up looking down across the land. A vertical line appeared between her eyes. She called softly to Ben, saying only his name. He did not look around nor reply as Town Marshal Gibbel raised his arm and slid his horse.

There were seven townsmen in the group. Two went on past, as far as the wagon, and sat there looking down, grim-faced and silent. Gibbel crossed his hands over the saddlehorn and squinted hard at Ben.

"Two of 'em got out," he said brusquely. "Old Will and Hal."

"Escaped?" Ben asked, stunned.

Gibbel nodded. "Yep. Bell's daughter visited 'em at the jailhouse, give Hal a pistol, he got the drop on Marshal Thomp-

184

son, and they broke out."

Ben regarded the older man for a long time without speaking. Finally he said, "What about El?"

"He didn't go with 'em. His arm's full of fever."

"And the girl — Bell's daughter?"

"Yeh, Hal took her along."

"The marshal?"

" 'Got a goose-egg on the back of his head, but otherwise in fair shape. Hal laid him out to give 'em time."

"How much of a start have they?" Ben asked.

"Not much; I seen 'em busting out of town and went down to Cliff's office an' found him sprawled out on the floor. After he come around I got up this posse and lit out after 'em. Their tracks lead west."

"Some horsemen crossed our trail going west not a quarter of an hour ago," Ben said.

"That'd be them." Gibbel looked past at the wagon. "Everything all right here?"

"Yes."

"Then I expect we'll be gettin' on," Gibbel said, reined around, called to his men, and struck out westerly in a rising cloud of dust.

Ben motioned for Joel to move out. He led all the way to Deming, left the horses at the liverybarn, told Sarahlee to take care of her grandfather, and hurried to Marshal Thompson's office. Cliff was bathing his head at the wash-stand when Ben came in. He looked around, grunted, and continued his ministerings. After a time he said, "I guess you heard."

"I heard. Are you fit to ride?"

"Yeah, in a minute." The marshal finished bathing the bruise on his head, poked it gingerly, then turned around. "Y'know, Ben, I think I made a helluva mistake. I should've let you shoot those two."

"You made a mistake all right," Ben said gruffly. "You should've leg-ironed both of them and put Della in with them."

Marshal Thompson put his hat on his head with extreme gentleness, rummaged through his desk for another six-gun, dropped it into his holster and gazed woefully at Ben. "Who'd have thought a lawyer's daughter'd do such a thing? They can't possibly get away with it, and now she's an accessory — or something." He moved towards the door, then stopped. "Maybe I'd better leg-iron Elbert."

"Never mind," Ben said, thrusting the door open. "If he didn't go with them when he had the chance, he's safe here for the time being. Come on; they've only got about an hour's jump on us."

Ben caught a flash of Sarahlee's face on the plankwalk as he and Marshal Thompson loped out of town. He threw up an arm and didn't look back. Riding westerly, the marshal pointed far ahead where a dust-banner was drifting lazily upwards near the first tier of trees. Ben urged his horse harder, found that it lacked the speed of his own chestnut, and swore aloud.

By the time they came to the first trees the posse was gone. Their tracks showed that they had stopped briefly, milled around, then had ridden on. Ben's face creased in a scowl. "They lost the tracks," he said to the marshal. "They're riding blind now."

"Don't worry; Jake's an old hand. If they went up that way he'll find 'em."

Ben shook his head and pointed to the west. "They aren't simple-minded enough to head right back where Will was taken, and short of circling around and going back to Deming, they've got only one other way to go."

"West," Marshal Thompson said. "All right, lead off."

The sun climbed and even in among the trees it was sticky-hot and listless. They had to keep urging their horses, riding zig-zag, quartering for sign, and finally, along to wards mid-afternoon, the marshal drew up and spat. "It's no use," he said, looking at the immense stillness around them. "They could be anywhere in here — or ten miles away. Without a trail we'll never find them."

They turned back, rode wearily back down to the prairie and flinched when the last shade was left behind. Ben set a course for the terminus of Roan's Creek. By the time they reached it the sun was glowing red above the western rim. They got down, slipped the bits, watered their animals, then stood in the shade smoking while their horses rested.

"Maybe Jake found 'em," Thompson said, with no conviction in his voice.

"Maybe. Maybe not, too."

"Where would they go?"

"I've got an idea," Ben said, exhaling mightily. "But it's a pretty wild one."

"The way I feel right now," the marshal retorted, "I want no more wild-goose chases." He sighed, removed his hat and felt the bump on the back of his head. "Dog-gone that Hal anyway; he didn't have to do that." He replaced the hat and smoked a while, watching the horses drowse in the shade. "I owe him something for that, and I'm a feller who always pays his debts."

"Speaking of debts," Ben said. "I wonder

how the judge made out today?"

"Probably about the way you think he did. Bell's your lawyer, and his tomfool girl's married to one of your opponents."

Ben dropped the cigarette and rowelled it with his spur. "You know, Cliff, the first time I saw her I thought she was one of the prettiest women I'd ever seen — and as hollow as a shell." He looked down the land towards Deming, eyes puckered nearly closed against the waves of heat. "Hal'll get all the punishment he deserves, just staying married to that woman."

"I hope she crowns him with an iron skillet," the marshal said, went to his mount, bridled it, snugged up the cinch and grunted up into the saddle. While he waited for Ben he said, "What'll you do if the judge rules against you, Ben?"

Roan mounted, turned his horse and joined the marshal in riding towards Deming. "Do? Why, I reckon I'll go down around Santa Fe and locate somewhere."

"Maybe in a dry-goods store?"

Ben looked around in puzzlement. "Dry-goods store? What're you talking about?"

"Didn't you know? Sarahlee's paw's got the biggest dry-goods store in the territory, over in Santa Fe."

"Well, he can keep it. I'll settle for four,

five hundred acres of fenced land adjoining some free-range."

"You've got that here."

"Not if the judge rules against me, I haven't."

"Hmmmm; after this is over, I reckon you'd be able to buy the Marlows out pretty cheap; then, ruling or no ruling, you could use that road till hell freezes over and for ten days on the ice."

"That bump must've done you more damage than you think. How could I buy the Marlows out? With what? They've got quite a spread up there — I've got three years' savings as a rider."

"You're forgetting something," the marshal said. "You've also got a damage suit against them for as much as you've got the guts to sue them for."

"Oh hell," Ben said in disgust. "That suing business is for a different breed of cats from my kind of folks." He patted his holster. "I prefer Judge Colt."

"Well, it doesn't look like you're going to get a chance to settle this by Judge Colt," Marshal Thompson exclaimed.

"Why not?"

"Because, as soon as I get back, I'm going to put two more posses out, then I'm going to wire the other towns hereabouts, and the next time you see the Marlows it'll be with their hands tied behind them."

"Maybe," Ben said.

CHAPTER NINE

Deming was exchanging its work-weary summer daylight garb for the release of nocturnal pleasures when Ben and the marshal rode into town. The shadows were long and darkening. Ben rode into the liverybarn with his mount and the marshal continued on down to his office. When Ben dismounted the nighthawk came forward with a limp.

" 'Evenin'," he said. "Damned horse kicked me in the knee, would y'mind off'saddlin' for me?"

Ben tugged the latigo loose, pulled the saddle and blanket off and turned. He was part way to the saddle-rack when a rifle exploded out in the roadway somewhere. He went down in a sprawl of leather and the hostler emitted a startled squeak, darted a look outside, then hobbled swiftly over to Ben.

" 'Ya hurt, Mister Roan?"

He put a hand on Ben's shoulder, then drew it back swiftly and sucked in his breath. A snout of a cocked pistol was looking up at him.

" 'T'wasn't me; hones' t'God, Mister Roan. Look, I got no gun."

Ben pushed the saddle aside and arose. He looked from the hostler to the roadway beyond, took several steps forward. The hostler's voice drew him back.

"Look here, Mister Roan."

The bullet had ploughed into the cantle of the saddle, broken the cantle-board and slashed the leather. Ben dragged the saddle over near a lantern and examined it. "Rifle," he said, worrying the flattened slug out with his pocket knife, and holding it in his hand. "Where was he, when he fired?"

"I don't know. I was jes' turnin' away with the horse when it come. I seen you go down and figured he'd drilled you sure."

"The force knocked me down," Ben said, studying the flattened bullet. He put it into a shirt-pocket and gazed out into the darkness. "I had an idea he'd be here in town, but it seemed too crazy to mention." He looked down at the saddle, holstered his pistol and swore. "There's fifty dollars shot to hell," he said. "Where does that back door lead to?"

"The alleyway. Want me to take a look around out there for you?"

"No; no sense in getting you shot for me," Ben replied, turning towards the rear of the barn.

"I'll get the marshal," the hostler called after him.

From the doorway Ben said, "Never mind, I'll take care of this without the marshal." He opened the door, studied the refuse-littered alley a long time, then slipped out into the darkness and made his way north through a litter of rubble until he came to a dog-trot between two buildings. There, he made his way back towards Deming's main thoroughfare. By the time he was in a position to see beyond the protective buildings, there was a little knot of men clustered around the hostler in front of the barn. The hostler was talking and gesticulating, and where the lamp-light struck his face, it showed up animated and flushed with excitement.

Across from Ben was the diner. South of that was the mercantile establishment; next to that was the narrow stairway leading to the rooms of the Oases Hotel above. Ben's glance lingered there a moment, probing the dark cavern of the opening, then they lifted and ranged along the blind row of windows overhead. All but two were open. The shots could have come from any of those windows. It could even have come from his own room. He thought it very likely that it had; that Will and Hal were up there; had been waiting for him. He thought that if they were up there they shouldn't have got impatient.

"Where is he?" A big voice boomed, over the murmur at the liverybarn. Ben looked south and saw Marshal Thompson thrusting into the crowd. The hostler said something and gestured towards the interior of the barn. Marshal Thompson looked, but did not enter.

Ben ducked back, went out through the alleyway northward until he came to the widely-spaced shacks near the end of the road, then trotted swiftly across to the east side of town. There, moving cautiously southward through another alley, he came down behind the diner. Several large tins of refuse there, reeking solidly, gave him protection while he studied the gloom beyond. He had hoped to find two saddled horses tied somewhere behind the Oases, but in this he was disappointed.

Distantly, men called to one another. One voice belonged to Marshal Thompson. Ben grimaced. All he needed was for Thompson to organise a man-hunt; he dared not show himself, and if he was seen skulking in the alley, the probability of some zealous towns-man shooting him was excellent. He edged along the backs of buildings until music from the Oases came through the partition, muted but distinguishable, then he looked for an opening which might lead to the rooms above. There was no rear entrance to the hotel, but there was an alley-entrance to the Oases. He entered, drew his six-gun and started along a dark passage when a door opened and a large, portly man looked straight into his face. The stranger's eyes grew wide and round; his body was motion-less.

"This isn't a robbery," Ben said. "Where's the inside stairway to the rooms above the saloon?"

"Listen, mister," the big man said. "I don't want no gunfights in here."

"Neither do I," Ben retorted. "Where's the stairway?"

"It's to your right there, beyond that door. But listen —"

"Mister, did you hear a rifle shot a little while back? Well, that was meant for me, and I think it came from out of the rooms upstairs."

The portly man's brows came down

slowly. "Oh," he said. "You must be Ben Roan."

"I'm not Governor Wallace, friend."

As Ben started past the big man said, "Wait a minute. I own this place. I'll get a shot-gun and go up with you."

"You'll stay down here," Ben said. "I don't like folks behind me with shot-guns."

When Ben opened the door it squeaked. Beyond, faintly lit by an untended and smoking lantern, the stairway leading up was dingy-looking and empty. He started to climb and nearly every board creaked under his weight. When his head was level with the hallway he stopped, listening. There wasn't a sound beyond, and behind him, too, there was an ominous silence; someone had silenced the pianist in the saloon. He was shifting his weight to take another step when he heard Marshal Thompson call to someone down in the roadway. Then, straight ahead and down the hallway, a door opened. Ben brought his cocked pistol up slowly. When a figure moved out he tilted the barrel just a fraction, held it there a second, then lowered it. The shadow moved closer to the hall-lamp and Ben recognised Sarahlee. Behind her, a man ambled into sight. His head was down and his bony outline was unmistakable: Doctor Brun-

197

dage. He said something to Sarahlee and started past. She nodded, watched him turn down the stair-well, then went back into the room. Ben felt a strong urge to call to her; to go to her room. His train of thought was interrupted by the sound of men in the passage below and behind him. He flattened against the wall, moved on up as far as the hallway, and faded into the darkness there.

Boots clumping up the stairs drove him into a little recess beside the stair-well's debouchement, and he pressed himself into the darkness there, waiting. Cliff Thompson was the first man to come into sight. Behind him was the Oases's owner, puffing from the climb and gripping a sawed-off riot-gun. Thompson twisted around and said, "Which room?"

The big man grunted back, "How do I know? They got no key from down stairs — they could be in any of them."

"Which is Roan's room?"

The big man thrust his shot-gun out. "That one; third from here on the left."

"Which did the girl get?"

The shot-gun moved. "Over here."

"You stay back here," Thompson said, starting forward. He went to the doorway of Ben's room, bumped it with his pistol barrel and stepped away. Only an echo came

198

back. He got bolder, reached down, lifted the latch and pushed inward. There wasn't a sound. From Ben's vantage place he saw the marshal suck in a big breath, exhale it, then jump through the door. His own gun was up and ready. The stillness drew out thin, then Cliff came back to the doorway, stuck his head out and said, "They aren't in here." His last word was drawn out slowly as his glance went to the doorway of Sarahlee's room. "I'll try that one."

As Thompson moved across the hallway the portly man shuffled a few steps forward and planted himself directly in front of Ben. Drawing himself up to see around the big man, Ben shifted his weight and the flooring protested. The big man started to twist around. Ben jammed the pistol into the small of his back and said, "Steady; don't move, mister."

"Roan?" The big man husked in a low tone. "It's the marshal; he's tryin' to find the feller who shot at you."

"I saw him. You just stand still and keep quiet."

"But, dammit, we're tryin' to help —"

"Shut up! I don't need your help."

The big man drew himself erect indignantly, but he was silent. Beyond him, Marshal Thompson rapped lightly on Sarahlee's door. When it opened he nodded. Ben couldn't see Sarahlee, but he could hear her voice.

". . . No, Marshal, I'm alone here with my grandfather."

"Did anyone try to get in here?"

"No."

"Have you seen your uncle or your cousin since you came back to town?"

"No; are they here — in Deming?"

"I think so. Didn't you hear a shot a little while ago?"

"I thought I did," Sarahlee replied. "When Doctor Brundage was here. But I didn't pay much attention."

"Ben rode back with me. Someone tried to pot-shoot him in the liverybarn."

"Oh . . ."

"He's all right, ma'm. Whoever it was, missed."

"Where is he?"

The marshal looked irritated. "I don't know, but I wish I did," he said curtly. "Sneakin' around town somewhere trying to find the bushwhacker, I expect."

"Marshal —"

"Now don't worry, Miss Sarahlee; I'll find him."

The saloon-owner started to move his head sideways. Ben jammed the gun hard into his back and he stiffened into immobility.

"Is your grandpaw all right?" Cliff asked.

"Yes; Doctor Brundage said he must be made of iron. All he needs is lots of rest. Marshal?"

"Yes'm?"

"Could you get a woman to come up here and watch him?"

"I reckon. What's on your mind?"

"I'd like to try and find Ben."

Thompson shook his head, hard. "No ma'm," he said with firm emphasis. "You stay right in this room, and if anyone wants to come in, you tell 'em to go on. Lock the door and put a chair behind it." When Sarahlee started to protest, Thompson frowned at her. "You just stay up here and watch the old man; as soon as I've found your uncle and cousin, I'll let you know. Now close the door, ma'm, and lock it."

Ben heard the door close. While the marshal was waiting to hear the lock click, Ben slid around the saloon owner, got to the stairways, and went downwards three steps at a time. Behind him the portly man shouted to Marshal Thompson. A quick look over his shoulder from the bottom of the stairs showed Ben the big outline of Thompson above him. As the marshal called his name, Ben slammed the door and hurried along the dark passage out into the alley. He had scarcely found cover in a dog-trot south of the Oases when the alleyway was filled with men and shouts.

Watching Marshal Thompson send details of men north and south, he waited until the last posseman had disappeared, then scuttled eastward across the alley to a high plank fence, went over it, and worked his way through the darkness to the intersecting alleyway, which ran east and west. There, with the moonlight beginning to soften the muddiness of shadows, he went swiftly eastward until he came to a darkened house, flanked by a coach-shed, a deserted chicken-house, and whose rear yard was surrounded by an old picket-fence, once white-washed, but now dirty grey and sagging.

He moved into the gloom near the chicken-house, stood there a long time studying the rear of the house, and when he was about to move closer, a whisp of movement near the back door arrested him.

A tall, lean shadow was leaving the house. Watery light shone dully off a carbine barrel. Ben smiled coldly to himself, waited until the shadow had hardened into the silhouette of a man, then he stepped out into plain sight.

"That's far enough, Hal," he said softly. "I figured you'd try to hide here."

Marlow froze, staring intently at the man down the yard from him, backgrounded by the chicken-house. "Roan!" he said, in a tight, soft tone of voice.

"Yeah, that shot hit the saddle I was carrying — not me."

"This one won't miss!"

"Hold it! You'd better not try it with a carbine, Hal."

Marlow was still and silent a moment, then he opened his fingers and the carbine fell at his feet. He moved his legs a little, taking a wider stance. His right arm drew back and upwards a little.

"Any time," Ben said.

"You're supposed to be a fast gun," Marlow half-whispered. "Let's see *how* fast!"

"Fast enough, Hal. *Go for it!*"

The first explosion came from Ben's gun, which hadn't moved six inches from the holster. Marlow stood there, wide-legged and staring, then he fired, but his barrel hadn't risen far enough and the slug went wide and low. He was straining to bring it higher when Ben's second shot spun him around. He staggered but did not go down.

Ben let the gun hang at his side. "Pick it

up," he said. "If that arm's numb use the other one. Go on, Hal — pick it up!"

Distantly, men cried out to one another. Behind them, a wavering lamp was being carried towards the rear of the house. Ben was aware of these things, but he didn't permit them to distract him.

"Pick it up, Hal!"

"No!"

Ben nodded coldly. "Turn around and head for the roadway," he said. When Hal hesitated, glaring, Ben drew his gun, raised it shoulder high, tilted back, and walked slowly forward. Hal turned and started around the house, holding his right arm with his left hand.

They were almost to the front gate when Ben drew off to one side, into the darkness of an angular shadow cast by the roofline, and let Delia Bell rush by to Hal. Then he moved up behind her.

"That's far enough, Hal. 'Evening, ma'm. He isn't hurt," Ben said, as Della, casting him one swift, frightened glance, reached her husband.

Men with lanterns were coming down the road. Ben watched them a moment, then said, "Hal, where's your paw?"

"Go to hell."

"Listen," Ben said sharply. "I don't want

to kill him any more than I wanted to kill you. Tell me where he is and I won't have to kill him."

"You won't get the chance," Hal said, looking around as the mob of townsmen came up, led by Cliff Thompson. "He's going to kill you, Roan."

"I guess he can try," Ben said, as Marshal Thompson moved past Hal towards him. "Howdy, Marshal. Sorry I couldn't hang around back at the hotel."

"Damn you, Ben, you're going to get somebody killed yet." He looked beyond Ben at the house. "Is the old devil in there?"

"Which 'old devil' do you mean? My lawyer or Will?"

"You know cussed well who I mean!"

"I haven't looked yet, Marshal." Ben turned, and Thompson caught his arm.

"Just a second. I'll go in there — you stay outside." As Thompson started towards the house he spoke over his shoulder to the townsmen clustered around Hal Marlow. "Take him down to the jailhouse and leg-iron him."

"What about her?" a cowboy asked.

Cliff stopped long enough to bend a long look at Della. "And her, too, doggone it."

"But — she's a woman, Marshal," the rider protested.

"That's not my fault," Thompson said. "Besides, she got Hal out and he busted me over the head, and I don't take kindly to being hit on the head. Leg-iron her, too."

A third voice, high and scratchy, broke in. Charley Bell came out of the shadows at the side of the house. "Just a minute, there," he said. "You can't lock my daughter up, Marshal."

Thompson squinted at the spritely figure. "Oh," he said. "It's you. I wondered when you'd crawl out from under the bed. Just give me one good reason why I can't lock her up."

"I'll get a writ. The judge's still in town. I'll —"

"You go get your writ, Bell, then I'll arrest you too."

"What? What for?"

"For aiding a jail-break — for harbouring criminals — for —"

"Wait a minute, Marshal. I had nothing to do with Hal coming here."

"Maybe not, but you sure weren't in any hurry to let me know he was here."

"I didn't have the chance. He'd only been here a few minutes when Roan came up."

Ben spoke up: "Mr. Bell, where's Will Marlow?"

Bell swung to face Roan. "I don't know,"

he said, and, as Ben continued to stare at him, he added: "Honestly I don't. Hal came in the back way and he was alone. Ask him if he wasn't."

"Do you mind if we search your house?" Ben asked.

The lawyer waved his hand towards the front door, "No, I don't mind. I'll even help you."

Ben started forward and again the marshal stopped him. "Hold it, Ben; like I said — you stay out here."

Ben shrugged, turned towards Hal, Della, and the possemen, and gazed steadily at the prisoner. "You can save your paw's life, Hal," he said. "Tell us where he is and I give you my word I won't throw down on him."

"Go to hell," the prisoner ground out.

Ben shrugged and Marshal Thompson told the possemen to take Hal to jail. As they were moving off, Ben went forward, touched Della's shoulder and when she turned, he motioned for her to come back inside the gate. She obeyed.

"Do your husband a favour," Ben said gently. "He doesn't want his father killed, but he's so full of hate right now he can't see straight. Tell us where Will is, Della."

"You heard what Hal said," Della replied,

looking into Ben's face with revulsion in her eyes.

"I heard. You also heard what I said. If we hunt him down he's going to get killed. He may get killed anyway, even if you tell us where he is. But you've got my word I won't draw against him, Della. The only way old Will's going to come out of this alive, is if you tell us where he's hiding so we can take him before he knows we're onto him."

"You give me your word you won't shoot him?"

"I give you my word," Ben said, and when Della continued to vacillate, he said, "I could've killed Hal — I didn't do it. Listen, Della; I don't want to kill the Marlows."

Charley Bell spoke to his daughter. "He's telling the truth, honey. You can trust him."

Marshal Thompson edged closer to the girl. "He could've killed Elbert, too — and he didn't."

Della looked down at the ground when she spoke. "All right, I'll tell you. He knows Mister Roan will go to the jailhouse sooner or later tonight. He's in the dog-trot between the apothecary's shop and the saddlery, across from the jailhouse."

Marshal Thompson blew out his breath. "Nice feller," he said. "Bell, I want your word you won't let this girl out of the house the rest of the night. If you don't promise, so help me, I'll lock her up."

"I promise, Marshal. I give my solemn word on it."

Cliff turned towards the gate. "Come on, Ben."

Deming's main thoroughfare was alive with men, all armed. The plankwalk in front of the Oases was dark with interested watchers, mostly riders from the big ranches. A hum of conversation filled the air, and down by the liverybarn a short, thickly made man with a plug hat and goatee, was standing slightly apart from a group of loungers. As Marshal Thompson stopped just short of the open roadway, he saw this plug-hatted stranger; touching Ben's arm, he said, "There's the judge. That's all we need right now."

Ben looked and grunted. "Looks like the whole blasted town's waiting for someone to get killed — the judge included." He leaned forward slightly to see around the corner. "Now, Marshal, I'm going to start across the road. You —"

"What!" Marshal Thompson said bluntly. "Are you crazy? You heard what Della said; that old buzzard's just waiting to pot you."

"Shut up and listen for a change," Ben said. "I'm going to walk out there and hit the dirt. When he fires you make sure he's in that dog-trot, then we'll plug up the front and rear of it, and make him surrender."

"Nossir, by God," Thompson replied emphatically. "You'll do no such a cussed thing. He wants you, not me; *I'll* walk out there and call him. You slip around through the alley and come into the dog-trot from the rear. Then, when he's listening to me, you throw down on him."

Ben was shaking his head before Thompson ceased speaking. His voice sounded patient when he spoke. "Cliff, you heard me give my word I wouldn't draw on him."

"Well — 'you going to let him kill you?"

"No, but —"

"Never mind the buts, dammit. I'll go." The marshal started forward. Ben moved swiftly behind him, grabbed him with both arms, swung him high and around and threw him down in the dust. When Thompson swore and clambered to his feet, Ben was already twenty feet out into the roadway and still walking. Cliff stared after him, started forward once, then swore, drew his pistol, and, instead of running to the alleyway, edged around the corner, got up onto the plankwalk and moved cautiously northward towards the dark pathway between the buildings where Will Marlow was crouched, waiting.

Somewhere up the moonlighted roadway a man called out. Ben turned. It was Cal Marlow, and he was hastening out of the darkness near the hotel's stairway into the road. A dark shadow Ben thought was Jake Gibbel came out of the marshal's office, looked up towards Cal Marlow, then twisted slowly and gazed quizzically at Ben. Suddenly, Gibbel dropped into a crouch. As he did so, Ben threw himself down. A rifle blasted into the hush; seconds later men were shouting.

Ben began to roll. The rifle exploded again and dust spurted over him. He leapt up and ran back the way he had come. The rifle went off the third time and Marshal Thompson roared a curse and leapt towards its protruding tip. The rifle wisped back out of sight into the dog-trot and Marshal Thompson, his forward momentum too strong to be checked, threw himself sideways and downwards. When the fourth shot came, the marshal was deafened by it. The bullet passed through the back of his jacket, through his shirt, and across Thompson's back, leaving an angry red welt.

Men were running towards the south end of town. Cal Marlow, well ahead, had a revolver in his fist. He was screaming something unintelligible; then he stopped, threw up the pistol and fired, and Cliff Thompson, drawing his body clear of the dark pathway between the buildings, heard Will's rifle fall, rattle along the siding and strike the earth. He got to his feet, picked up his pistol and moved, white in the face, directly into the maw of the dog-trot.

Ben, seeing the marshal going in, lunged for him, caught his arm and pulled him away a fraction of a second ahead of a thunderous pistol shot. Thompson swore and aimed a blow at Ben, who ducked under it and darted forward. The marshal's gun was still up, cocked and ready, as Ben went down low, almost against the ground, and into the dog-trot. Cliff leapt after him, saw the blue-black sheen of a pistol dropping down, and fired at the indistinct shape behind it. The lowering pistol went off, Ben fell back against the marshal's legs, and Thompson staggered.

Someone was clawing at Ben to get past him. He reached up blindly, caught the man, and with a tremendous heave, threw him back out of the dog-trot. Marshal Thompson's gun lanced the darkness a second time, and the black form beyond, staggering back, bent in the middle and went down.

Thompson's breath was rasping in and out. He grabbed Ben's shoulder and lugged him back onto the plankwalk, then he bent, got Ben under both arms, and heaved him upright.

"Where'd it hit you?" he asked, peering closely at Ben's face, covered by both hands.

"It didn't," Ben said from behind his palms, "the muzzle-blast damned near blinded me. Did you kill him?"

"Deader'n seven hundred dollars, all spent," Cliff said, and turned angrily when someone kept tugging at his elbow. "What the hell do *you* . . . Oh, hullo, Judge."

"Who was that, in there, Marshal?" the judge asked, peering into the darkness beyond.

"Will Marlow — the man who tried to close the Roan Creek road."

"I see. And this man here?"

"This is Ben Roan. His father made that damned road."

"Is he badly hurt?"

"He says not," the marshal replied, "but we'd better get Doc Brundage to make sure."

Ben put his hands down and blinked wetly at the gathering crowd of men. "I'm all right," he said. Someone held out a clean, folded white handkerchief. Ben took it,

213

looked at the donor, and nodded. "Thanks, Mister Marlow — I'm sorry about your brother."

Cal Marlow went to the edge of the dog-trot and looked in. "I am too," he said soberly. "It couldn't have ended any other way, though, young man."

The judge shouldered closer and peered up at Ben. "Was the shooting over that road?" he asked.

Ben dabbed at his eyes a moment before he replied. "Partly; it started out that way."

"I see. Well, the road's been declared open, Mister Roan. You have full right of access."

"I'm obliged, Judge."

"Not at all," the judge said a trifle stiffly, and moved on past.

Jake Gibbel elbowed through with Doctor Brundage. As the medical man examined Ben's face, the Town Constable said, " 'Y God, I seen him poke the rifle barrel out, and it sure took me by surprise."

"I'm glad it did," Ben replied. "When I saw you duck, I hit the road. If you hadn't ducked when you did he might've got me, Jake."

Doctor Brundage growled, "Hold still."

The marshal re-loaded his gun, holstered it, and turned to the crowd. "Couple of you boys lug him out through the alley and over to Doc's embalming shed." As several men edged around Ben and into the dog-trot, the marshal, seeing someone familiar hurrying up, broke through the crowd and caught Sarahlee before she got close. "Ben's all right, so you just simmer down," he said, keeping hold of her arm. "Ol Man Marlow's dead — and the judge gave Ben right of access up to his folks' place."

"Let me go to him, Marshal."

Cliff drew her back and turned her round. "You go on back to his room and wait. I'll bring him to you."

"But he —"

"No buts, Miss Sarahlee. It's all over. Do like I say, and I'll fetch him to you. Now go on."

Sarahlee went, and the marshal watched her until she disappeared into the hotel stairway, then he raised his voice to the men milling around in front of him. "Dammit! Don't you fellers have homes? Go on, now; get off the road!"

When only the three of them remained, Doctor Brundage wiped his hands on a limp handkerchief and scowled at the marshal. "That was a tomfool thing to do; let this man walk out there when the whole town knew Marlow was waiting to kill him."

"Let him," Thompson said loudly. "Why, he went out there by himself and after I'd told him not to."

Brundage gazed at Ben a moment, seemed about to say something, then turned abruptly and walked away.

Ben blinked away the tears which had formed over his eyeballs, and grinned at the lawman. "Funny how folks see things, isn't it? He's probably not the only one in Deming who believes you engineered me out into the roadway for a target."

"Damn you anyway," the marshal swore. "That's all this mess needs — a lying ending."

"Don't worry; I'll tell folks how it was. Say, about El and Hal . . ."

"I'll explain to them — but I think that was the dumbest thing a man ever did, Ben — not drawing your gun."

Ben looked up the roadway where groups of men were talking. "No it wasn't," he said slowly. "I'm going to marry Sarahlee, Cliff. If I'd killed her uncle it would have always been between us."

"Not in self-defence," Thompson said stoutly. "Anyone'd understand that."

Ben shook his head, turned, and started towards the hotel stairway. Men watched

him pass in silence and the soft-silver
moonlight shone dully over the town.